BOAT NUMBER FIVE

THE SLOVAK LIST

BOAT NUMBER FIVE

Monika Kompaníková

TRANSLATED BY
JANET LIVINGSTONE

LONDON NEW YORK CALCUTTA

The Slovak List
SERIES EDITOR: Julia Sherwood

This book has received a subsidy from SLOLIA Committee,
the Centre for Information on Literature in Bratislava, Slovakia

Seagull Books, 2021

First published in Slovak as *Piata loď*
© Monika Kompaníková / LITA, 2010

First published in English by Seagull Books, 2021
English translation © Janet Livingstone, 2021

ISBN   978 0 8574 2 889 9

British Library Cataloguing-in-Publication Data
A catalogue record for this book is available from the British Library.

Typeset by Seagull Books, Calcutta, India
Printed and bound in the USA by Integrated Books International

This story is deeply grounded in the everyday reality of Slovakia as experienced from the point of view of a young person. I have tried to be true to the atmosphere and style of the original work. That is to say, it was written from inside the head of a young girl, whose thoughts are a stream that flows in a slow jumble, one after the other. The names of the characters have been preserved in the original form and not altered to a form that would be easier for an English-language reader to pronounce in their head. The most challenging, in this sense, is the main character's name—Jarka. Jarka is short form of the name Jaroslava and in Slovak is pronounced 'Yahrka'.

I wish you a truly heartfelt journey through Jarka's world.

*

This translation was made possible by the generous support of Renáta Bláhová in Bratislava, Slovakia.

Boats float through my dreams often. Boats that look like figures in a cartoon where anything can happen. They are skeletal, fashioned from thick, roughhewn boards. The gaps between the ribs of the hull are filled in with putty and all the flaws are covered with a coat of cobalt blue or opaque white. They seem fragile and unstable, but affable. Sometimes they have a cabin where you can hide, sometimes they're just empty shells without oars or lines. They drift on the surface, in still water with no current, without wind. When I wake up, I'm sweaty and tired, and my arms hurt. I feel like I've put out so much energy yet got nowhere, neither bottom, nor port. The undercurrents haven't caught me, and the wind is whirling, imprisoned in some valley, far from the water.

I saw boats for the first time almost 20 years ago during a nap. It left behind more of a feeling than an image, a hint of nausea.

I was in the garden, lying on the grass, playing a simple game of stamina and patience. The dry August stalks of grass pricked me through my T-shirt, and I had to stay in that uncomfortable position until I had some sign that I could get up. The sign would be anything ordinary and unforeseen—a leaf falling to the ground, the edge of a shadow joining with a stone, a blackbird whistling. If it happened, I would move and scratch myself, if not, I'd keep lying there without moving. I was waiting for the sound of metal scraping on metal, for a train taking the curve below the garden plots. Until that trusty and familiar sound could be heard, I couldn't move. The stalks were as sharp as needles, but I didn't move an inch—I stuck it out, my arms flung out to the sides, hidden among the blades of grass, palms turned to the sky. I felt an ant crawling on my palm. I flinched a little, the ant crawled off, and for a moment I lost myself in time and space. I felt like I was lying on the bottom of a boat that was drifting and lulling me to sleep. Sleep within sleep. Through my half-closed eyes, I saw only the blue sky, clear and sparkling, the sides of the boat and one oar above me, set across the hull. When it's time to wake up, I can grab the oar and pull myself up, I think. When will it be time to get up?

Then the slowly creeping shadow of the garden hut shaded my eyes and I felt that someone was standing over me. I was disoriented for a moment but felt safe. I turned my head, blinked and looked up. There wasn't anyone standing there, just an apple tree and just beyond it the garden hut. The apple tree was swaying, and the movement of the tree fit perfectly into my dream. It looked thick and full of branches because every leaf was doubled by a shimmering shadow created in my eye. The unripe apples hung on the branches like small decorations, misfits with nowhere better to be. But it was enough to blink and rub my eyes with my fingertips and the apple tree's true fecundity returned. Looking at the apples I realized that I had eaten almost nothing that day. I propped myself up on one elbow and closed my eyes again for a moment. I could have lain motionless for another half-hour, maybe even two hours, if I'd really wanted to. If I'd had a reason, if someone had made a bet with me, for example. For example, a bet for a roll or some hot cocoa. For that I would have done anything then. I was twelve years old.

I sat up and looked up and down and side to side to relax my stiff neck. Then I reached back and felt a circle of packed-down soil in the grass that looked like a place where a barrel had been rolled away after many years.

The memory is shockingly vivid. I remember how I went over the soil several times with my palm. I pushed down anything that was sticking out and made it even with my fingers. I also remember how I turned over and looked for a long time at that empty place, as if I wanted to remove all doubt that it was really there or assure myself that I had not dreamt it. I could have dreamt about the boat and about that small grave. I could have dreamt that I was dreaming about the grave, because that kind of thing happens sometimes. A person lies there thinking and falls asleep. They sleep for an hour or two.

Lucia, my mother Lucia—since I was little, she had told me not to call her Mama, I feel like some old cow—used to fall asleep like that often. Her eyes half-closed, two moist black slits. Curled up in a ball, her legs underneath her, sometimes without moving, and other times with her eyeballs moving back and forth, from left to right. Then she would emerge from the couch, like from mud, like a shadow of my real, live and capable mama. You can't be tired when you've slept for two hours, I told her. She would protest, claiming that she hadn't been sleeping, just resting and reading the teletext. She would answer me slowly and breathlessly or just whisper and squint so that I would believe her. So that, before I ran outside, I would put some more water in the electric kettle and fix her a strong Turkish coffee.

A few handfuls of dirt covered a dead cat squashed into the ruts in the road by a tyre in front of the neighbour's garden gate. It lay there, still warm, it's fur dusty and one leg unnaturally broken. A motorcycle had divided it into two equal halves, but if it hadn't been for that one wayward, shining bead popped out of its eye socket, the cat would have looked like it always did—stretched out on the road, lazy, self-satisfied and indifferent to my meddlesome attention.

I couldn't protect myself from an urgent need to look at it and I fought with an urge to take a stick, knife or garden shears and fish around inside its cracked-open chest. I was curious about what was under the fur, what it felt like to the touch, how it smelt. Whether it's like the meat in the school cafeteria or a cut finger. So, I covered it with some dirt and gravel from the road.

When I was seven years old, my friends and I buried a sparrow. We found him under the balcony in the housing complex, a pink tangle with a few wet feathers and enormous blue eyelids. It was hard to believe that such a thing would some day fly away or be fun to watch as it pecked at crumbs in front of the supermarket. We chose a nice, quiet place for it, and dug a hole three fingers deep. We built a miniature tombstone out of two pencils and a stone—a stone and a cross, as it should be, as is done when they bury a person. We gave it a real funeral too. We put on our dark tracksuits and brought flowers and slim birthday candles and recited the children's bedtime prayer. Those who didn't know the prayer got to join in at least for the last few syllables, but every one of us caught a whiff of death and the awareness of its irrefutability.

A week later we found some other thing to keep us busy and forgot about the sparrow.

I was alone when, four or five years later, I stood over the dead cat in front of my garden gate. Without friends who would reflect my own uncertainty, without faith in guardian angels, without real sorrow for cats that never wanted to be stroked.

I took a thorough, close-up look at the cat and didn't feel anything unusual, neither regret nor sadness. It wasn't my friend, it was only a moocher who appeared as soon as I pulled out some food and who never thanked me for it. I tried to shed a tear, but it didn't work. I tried not to look at it, but that didn't work either.

So, I returned to the garden, took the broom from behind the garden-hut door and started sweeping the room so that I could think about something else. I went all the way to the gate with the pile of dust I had swept up onto some old newspaper and couldn't resist a quick look at that black smudge on the road. Then I shook out the blankets and cushions and, when I thought someone was calling me from behind the hedge, I threw the cushions onto the grass and ran out through the gate. But there was no one, again just that black smudge, a black hole attracting curious girls. Finally, I took the shovel and, on the third or fourth try, managed to shovel it up off the ground. I walked around for a bit in front of the gate with the heavy shovel, thinking about whether to throw it over the fence into the neighbour's yard, but then I decided to part with it in a slightly more dignified way.

The sparrow's funeral had been a secret ritual. Our common fear confirmed our friendship. Each one of us did something for the sparrow, wordlessly and without the usual arguing, without complaining and cursing, in the conviction that this task that had fallen upon us directly from the heavens and was truly important.

Burying a cat was work like any other—dirty and strenuous. The shovel was too heavy for me, and by the time I had walked around the hut, the apple tree and the flowerbeds, I had used up so much strength that I dropped the body from the shovel onto the ground by mistake and saw its other, less preserved side. I couldn't decide where to bury it. I took a nice white stone from a pile of gravel on one side of the hut, walked away and threw the stone backwards over my shoulder. Where the stone fell I dug a hole with a children's shovel. Then I took the cat, put it back on the big shovel and placed it carefully into the hole as if I were putting dough into a baking mould. I carefully wiped the shovel off with some grass and put it back into the tool shed. I filled in the hole, smoothed it over and planted a clump of grass on top, which I had dug up from the same spot before. I tramped on it so that it wouldn't stick up too much, but it still looked funny. In the end, I pulled the trampled grass out again and threw it over the fence into the neighbour's garden, relying on the natural expansiveness of weeds.

No one ever looked for the cat, not even the one who ran over it with his motorcycle, or the neighbours who came only seldom to the garden at that time, only when something was ripe. Even I didn't miss it, not that specific cat, because there were a lot of them wandering around, and when one of them disappeared, another turned up in two days. I knew that sooner or later another one would saunter in and be there licking itself, purring and winding itself around my legs. It would be enough if I left an unwashed bowl, a bone or a piece of a roll in front of the hut door. Cats are like fruit flies that are born the moment the first drop of wine hits the bottom of the glass. They'll appear and scratch patiently at the door and meow. And when they get a piece of food, they'll take off. They'll find themselves a hole in the fence or crawl under the gate or walk around calmly and importantly with their tail sticking up as a sign of disdain for the children who felt sorry for them and shared their afternoon snack.

When I left, I always carefully closed the latch and locked the door to the hut and the garden gate. I put on my sweatshirt, shook the crumbs out of the pockets and started down the hill along the rutted road. When it rained, the ruts got deeper, and the water washed the stones and sand out of them. I stopped for only a brief moment at the place where the motorcycle had passed. I didn't feel anything unusual while doing it, neither disgust, nor sorrow. Boredom and hunger urged me on.

Lucia was home, there was a light on in the kitchen, I saw it from far away. With joyful relief I started running again, and for the last 100 metres I took great leaps, like Simon Says, or 'who's got the golden arm? YOOOOU do!', like the games we used to play in the courtyard. Hopscotch, Bloody Knee and others.

The stairwell was dark, only the long row of doorbells and names by the entrance was lit and made the way home shorter. The front door wasn't completely shut because someone who had gone out for a cigarette or to the corner shop hadn't felt like taking their keys with them. To avoid the door slamming, you had to close it very carefully, holding it open with your leg so the lock didn't click into place, or you had to stick a folded junk-mail flyer between the door and the frame to keep it from locking. Lucia used to leave the front door open a crack when she was expecting someone and didn't feel like coming down from the third floor. She always tensed up strangely when she was closing the door slowly, with her head down between her hunched-up shoulders like a turkey, her hair falling over her face. Through her flowing hair, you could see only one alert eye, trained on the enemy territory of the common hallway, where the neighbours peeped out of their doors. She left the door open a crack by jamming one of my tennis shoes into it from inside so that the draught wouldn't make it slam and her friends could come into the flat without knocking whenever they felt like it. Often, they didn't even take off their shoes and acted like they were in some public waiting room where someone came early in the morning to sweep up and empty the ashtrays. In a waiting room, the doors don't lock, shoes are not taken off, you spit on the floor and there's chewing gum stuck to the bottom of the chair. You come in hesitantly, with expectations, and leave in a rush without saying goodbye. Just like at our house.

I always had to take off my shoes, even if I was just going to the other end of the hall for my coat, otherwise I got smacked upside the head. Everybody else was an exception. Lucia never said anything to them about their muddy shoes, she just gaped at them in shame. She was embarrassed that she couldn't keep her own flat clean or set some rules. Maybe she didn't care and the only one she raised her hand and voice against was me, because I was hers, I was part of her and with me it was OK.

Lucia was afraid of Grandma Irena too. Even when Irena was lying almost helpless in bed and needed to have her diapers changed and her food pureed. Lucia let herself be ordered around and lectured to by her mother. Even though she knew that Irena was wrong and was asking her to do things that didn't make sense, she did everything to a 't', just to keep the peace, so there wouldn't be a fight. Someone who didn't know our family situation could interpret it as love, as care for an old, sick mother. A service, which should be natural, but wasn't, because the relationship between Lucia and Irena was purely business. Lucia's relationship to both of us was commercial, not familial. No deep affection, rapport or understanding. Not even a hint of intimacy or closeness.

She was capable of being nice to me, as long as I behaved the way she wanted and didn't cause her any problems. If you're not good, don't say your mine, she often said to me. Do what you want. Do what you want, Jarka! But don't come to me with your problems, understand?

Irena once said to Lucia: You will change my sheets and I'll let you live in my flat. Otherwise, you'll have to wait for it. Don't try to fool me, I'm still sharp.

A family operating on the principle of barter. Nothing good ever came of these little business deals.

I worked off every look from Lucia. Jarka, don't make trouble, otherwise I won't love you, she used to say. And so I anxiously tried not to cause any trouble. I just tried to make everything work the way Lucia wanted. I read the wishes on her lips so I could fulfil them even before she spoke them out loud. But her wishes were usually so crazy that I didn't understand them and couldn't fulfil them. I knew how to shop, clean, hang the laundry on the line, take the crate of empty bottles back to the local grocers. At the same time, I brought home 'A's from school and knew how to stay in my room for two days and pee into a pot.

Other children were still playing their games with pretend brooms, pretend pots, pretend soap, pretend money. For us, there was no pretending.

If the front door of the building was closed, Lucia's friends would ring and ring and push all the buzzers in a row. When one of the cursing neighbours would open up for them, they would come up to the flat and knock and pound on our door. They used our bathroom and towels, even my small ones that hung lower to ground on a special rack, on the tail of a plastic doggie. They came into my room, lay down on my bed, drunk and out of control, and I often had nowhere to sleep. In my room, they left behind a stench, muddied sheets, sometimes a lighter or small change that fell out of their pockets.

One of them, Lucia's favourite guy called Engineer who got work for her, would lie down in my bed even when I was in it. He'd come at night or at dawn, when he thought I was sleeping, always when there was a party at our place and lots of people and he could easily slip out of Lucia's sight. He would carefully close the door behind him, take off his shoes, kick them under the bed, take off his T-shirt and pants, put a hand over my mouth and another between my legs. He breathed hard and fast like a tired dog and his breath smelt like cigarettes and a wet rag someone had left in the corner. I would just close my eyes tightly and open my mouth so my soul could come out. I would imagine that I was swimming underwater. Swimming, and everything I felt—his touch, saliva, breath—came from the water, reeds and creatures living in the water. I didn't make a sound, didn't move, I never did anything, I just quietly left my body. When he finished, he would close the door behind him, and I would emerge from the water, return, change my clothes and sheets and go back to sleep.

By morning, I had put him out of my head enough to sit at the table with him and Lucia and have a breakfast. When I met him outside in the housing complex, I would pretend that nothing had happened, that I didn't remember or recognize him. Often I didn't remember anything specific, nothing terrible or painful that would stand out, just a vague feeling of dirtiness and shame. Like when a man in the bus told me I stank and that it wasn't fitting for a girl like me. No, but a big, sweaty man isn't fitting for a girl like me either.

I couldn't add to Lucia's troubles by coming and telling her there was a man I didn't like lying in my bed while another one was doing her in the room next door. She wouldn't listen to me or believe that I, such a young girl, could have any problems. Your problems, Jarka, aren't problems. They're just stupid stuff, she would say. Stupid stuff, stupid stuff.

Her friends, they were a whole battalion of guys from the juvenile-reform school, all crude gestures and talk, scars on their forearms and souls, who could burst into tears over a plate of plum dumplings, because their most beautiful memories from childhood were linked to plum dumplings. A minute later they were capable of smashing the empty plate against the wall or demonstratively slitting their wrists. And Lucia soaked it up like a sponge. She took something from each one of them—for a while she listened to jazz, then film soundtracks. Sometimes she would burn incense, other times she moved the furniture around according to the rules of Feng Shui. Then she started to smoke in the kitchen and bathroom, throwing the butts into the toilet where they would still be floating around two days later, and she would put the dirty shoes into the laundry basket and the dirty laundry in the closet. She learnt how to drink shots followed by wine and mix liquids with medicines, she learnt how to stick her finger down her throat when needed. She would lie there like a rag, sweaty, damp and sometimes dirty, because there were days when she was so tired that she didn't have the strength to go into the bathroom and wash.

I imagined some kind of worm or tapeworm that travelled through her veins into her heart and nested there, sucking her strength and emotions. I imagined a tapeworm because I didn't see any other reason why Lucia should be constantly tired and unable to do simple things like deal with basic hygiene. She was very young then, after all, younger than all my friends' mothers. When she went for the first and last time to a parent–teacher meeting, the teacher didn't want to tell her anything because she didn't believe she was my mother. I myself didn't address her as Mama and it confused the teacher—she had never met anyone like that. So my mother never went back to the school after that, she got her information by telephone. I was a First Grader and she wasn't even twenty-five yet. She looked like my sister.

When I was born, Lucia was sixteen. It's quite understandable that she wasn't happy about it. Becoming a mother at that age could only mean one thing for her—getting old, being stuck at home, in the flat, sitting around, gaining weight, not taking care of yourself, losing friends, lovers, interest in life, free time, sleep and freedom. So she fought it with all her strength. When she went somewhere, she would dress like my classmates in short pink or purple skirts and T-shirts with latex lettering. Sometimes she would squeeze into tight jeans and big men's tennis shoes and wear a hood or baseball cap. On her arms would jangle cheap, hammered bangles that fell down over her wrists. She'd walk with her fingers clenched up like claws, like the end of a rake, so she could keep them on her wrists. We could exchange clothes, wear the same shoes, go shopping together—if we liked the same things—and it was worth it to Lucia.

Don't call me Mama, she said over and over again, I feel like an old cow when you do. Call me Lucia. But the name just wouldn't come out of my mouth. It always got caught somewhere in my throat. But I learnt how to do that too.

But you are my mama, I thought. Aren't you? It's always clear who the mother is, isn't it? Not everyone has to know. Are you ashamed of me?

Stop talking nonsense! I'm tired.

I'm tired—the last word of every conversation.

Fatigue didn't suit her, though. She was so young. I remember just before Irena died and we didn't have to go from one rented flat to another anymore or put up with Irena's explosive temper. I knew how to take care of myself fairly well, I spent a lot of time in after-school activities and after-school care. Lucia had a relatively stable job, which meant that she worked for about three months in one place, she had a relatively stable relationship, which meant that the man in question was willing to fix the broken flush mechanism on our toilet and his toothbrush was sitting on the sink. From those times I remember Lucia as lively, merry, bouncing around the flat, I even remember how she cooked and cleaned and shopped and all the normal things that mothers do at home. And only when she was really stressed—an argument with a friend, a late salary payment—would she stand by the window, stamp her foot and tap her long thumbnail against the even longer nail on her index finger to the rhythm of some song. We had inherited a small flat. Irena was dead and for us it was an incredible miracle.

Irena's husband, a certain Mr Miletic who was also my grandfather, left for Austria in 1968, right after the Soviet invasion. Everyone was very surprised by this, because Mr Miletic had been the silent type his whole life—a calm, reliable and non-confrontational worker. One day he went to the cemetery in Devin, which is near the border with Austria, to pull up weeds from his brother's grave, and he never came back. About two or three years later, a postcard arrived and then nothing, the earth closed up. He had left his wife and two-year-old daughter in Bratislava. If Irena, with affected self-denial, talked about him, she only referred to a Mr Miletic whose arms were always dirty up to his elbows with soil. I myself never knew him, didn't know anything more about him except that he was a servile and indecisive weakling, had a garden and spent all his free time there. There or at the Devin cemetery.

Irena was the director of an elementary school and when she got pregnant, just before turning forty, and it must have been quite a blow. Until then, she had been well-known as an old maid who had sacrificed her body and mind to the education of socialist youth, and now she had to marry the maintenance man from the Dimitrovka factory and take care of the child from her own unwanted pregnancy. After the first six weeks of life, the child travelled to the crib at the day-care centre, which was part of the school under the auspices of the director's office and, every three hours on the dot, got a bottle of formula and some antiseptic powder on her bottom. Irena handled a career and a family in exemplary fashion, until a certain Mr Miletic decided to weed his brother's grave. Then one day, they moved Comrade Director to the kitchen in the very basement of the concrete building, because the wife of an emigrant is not suitable for making the children into proper communists.

They had degraded her, checking out her background as if she were some suspicious character. She suddenly grew old, and the evil nestled inside her came out. She shut herself up in the apartment in a voluntary quarantine. Three days after this fall from grace, she cleaned the flat so thoroughly that there was no trace of Grandpa left, not even a matchstick forgotten between the mattresses. She cleaned her concrete bunker and perfected her daily regime. It was no longer interrupted by any maintenance men. The spoons and forks were placed on paper napkins as if for the high-school ball, and never-used, decorative cloth napkins aesthetically arranged by colour. Everything strictly by tone, arranged as straight as a ruler.

In Neudorf, 10 kilometres beyond the Austrian border, there is a big flower shop called Miletich. I think I should go there sometime and look around. At the flowers, the sprouted vegetables for planting and the bulbs.

Fifteen years later, Irena did a similar cleaning, as thoroughly as the first time. She cleaned up after my Lucia and me. I went back to work after six weeks, why shouldn't you, Irena decided. Find yourself a place to live as soon as possible, you can stay with the baby in the kitchen until you find something. Three months, not one day more. You've destroyed my life, I don't want to see you here anymore. Take what you need from your room, I'll take care of the rest. I'll lock the room so you know there's nothing left in there.

Then Irena, without mercy, threw away Mama's stuffed animals, blocks, children's books, all her children's things, everything that Lucia didn't pack up or hide. And she took almost nothing with her because she didn't take Irena seriously.

On Christmas 1989, Irena gathered in a box all the official papers, stamps, badges, flags, party congress minutes, and souvenirs from the organized recreation events—simply everything demonstrating that she had been an active communist. Then she celebrated a Christian Christmas with everything that went with it, as if she'd been doing it behind closed doors all along. When she smelt danger, she acted like a hermaphrodite snail—she turned into something else and crawled tirelessly on through the mud.

We returned to Irena's house when she was around sixty-five and had a broken hip. At that time, it probably seemed to her like the most economic and logical solution. After all, who else should take care of her and give back to her everything that she had given years before. Who else than her daughter and granddaughter? After all, her granddaughter was already capable of carrying heavy loads and counting change in a shop. Lucia accepted this, because she no longer knew where to go—nine years moving from one rental to another was enough. She cast her eyes down, unpacked her bags and thus accepted her defeat. After a week, I understood that any alternative to this holy trinity would have been better, but Lucia said that we had to hold on, that even wicked old witches die.

Don't call me Grandma, she warned me right at the beginning, when we already knew what was what. Do I look like a Grandma to you? She asked, offended. Actually no, I thought to myself. I imagined a Grandma to be completely different—kindly and soft, with a wide embrace. I'll call you old hag.

Call me Irena. I told you that a long time ago. I'm no Grandma to you. Or anyone else.

Yes, ma'am!

So I lived with Lucia and Irena. They could easily have been two older babysitters. I could just as easily have been living with the neighbours.

Until then we had lived in a rental at the other end of the city, in a four-room flat with six or seven students from some arts academy. I never saw them all together in one place, and their faces all blurred into one puddle of colour. I got the impression that they would lend each other clothes, shoes, cologne, partners and thoughts, that they had one common closet from which they pulled whatever they liked, without regard for gender or size. They were fun and mostly good-natured, but it was tiring to follow their comings and goings, moods and quarrels. Often they would exchange bedrooms and beds. At night, a guy with a shaved head would go into one bedroom and come out of a different one in the morning. Or a stranger would come and take someone's place, someone who had disappeared without a word, someone I had just got used to. I had the feeling that we were living in a plastic dollhouse where some nasty child was constantly moving the furniture around.

We had no privacy or peace. Lucia and I slept together on a narrow bed in a miniature room, which from time to time served as one roommate's dark room and another's ceramics workshop. When Irena made her generous offer to us, Lucia didn't hesitate and wrote off her security deposit and the penalty for breaking the lease.

To somehow camouflage her gnawing feeling of having given in, Lucia raged like a tornado and immediately began to reorganize the flat.

Irena had to move onto the couch in a crowded and narrow living room while the two of us began to enjoy the luxury of a large, well-lit bedroom. Lucia moved the television into the bedroom and left Irena the radio, having intentionally removed its antenna. Lucia shoved her pantyhose in between the towels, changed the radio station, poured the silverware into one slot in the silverware holder and threw away the glass carps and swans. Irena's long-conceived and precisely organized system fell apart within a few days.

This is a circus! Shouted Irena. No order, no system! Everything is ruined! You've ruined absolutely everything . . . She suffered like an animal, but she was powerless, she couldn't do a thing, just hold onto the door or me, smooshing my shoulder and piercing the carpet with her cane. She couldn't even raise her crutch high enough to send the towels flying around the room.

Irena made needlepoint pictures. Cross-stitched, embroidered still-lifes with fruit and bouquets of lilacs, dusty, faded. One day, Lucia took all of Irena's pictures down from the wall and began to strip them mercilessly of their frames. Irena stood in front of me like an old collapsed smokestack, a pile of rubble, leaning with one hand on the doorframe and trying with the other to pull the unframed canvases to her with the crutch. Her knees were shaking and the crutch just rubbed along the carpet. In school they endlessly taught us that we should respect our elders, give up our seat for them and help them with their grocery bags. At that moment I saw her anger up close and her face disfigured by helplessness, her lashless eyes watery and red, her yellow skin that reminded me of a piece of wrinkled wax paper from the butcher. I saw her thinning hair lacking its silver lustre, her scars, the hairs growing on her face, her liver spots and tendons. She was unpleasantly real, and I looked at her like an insect magnified under a microscope. I smelt the unmistakable odour of an ageing body and saw nothing else in her but an old witch reaching out with her claws so she could stick them into my shoulder and use me like another limb.

Once, as Irena was trying to get at Lucia with her crutch, the hand that was holding onto the doorframe slipped. Instinctively she turned to me, reached out her liver-stained hand, stretching out her fingers like a bird of prey ready to swoop down on some small rodent. I jumped back in horror, ran past Lucia and out into the hall. I heard a low thud, but maybe I just imagined it.

We divided up a flat that was full of neatly stored junk.

First, we got rid of everything that reminded us of Irena, her personal possessions, clothing, vases, figurines and the pictures that Lucia hadn't managed to destroy the year before. Her clothes, made from synthetic fabric from socialist East German factories that couldn't even be used as rags, we stuffed into plastic bags and left by the dumpsters. For weeks afterward, we found Irena's suits, towels, nylon curtains and pantyhose strewn across the housing complex, caught in trees or wet in the gutter by the road.

When we were cleaning Irena's things out, we decided—Lucia decided—to throw out the awful cupboards covered in oak veneer that creaked scarily and swayed, even though they were standing on wooden boards. I was afraid that one day when I was taking some socks off the top shelf, it would fall on me and cut me in two and Lucia wouldn't have the strength to lift it off and rejoin my torso with my legs.

Someone took the cupboards away during the night. And the dismantled double bed from which we kept only the mattresses. The night tables with their hinges ripped off hung around the yard for two weeks until the neighbour from the ground floor took them to the third floor and left them in front of our door with a note asking us to dispose of our junk properly, at the junkyard. Then we stealthily, week after week, got rid of the big overstuffed bags whenever the garbage collectors had already emptied the dumpster. After dark, so that the neighbours wouldn't notice.

After Lucia's rampage, the flat was totally destroyed. She lost interest in it and just used the advantages that it offered. The big plan to renovate the devastated space was then postponed from November to December and from December to summer. There still wasn't enough money or time, and even though Lucia's wide circle of friends continued to grow, there wasn't anyone who could come with their big car and take us to a store to buy the furniture we needed and carry it up to the third floor. I didn't mind that we had got rid of Irena's things, but I had counted on implementing the original, ambitious plan, which included a bed, a desk, a cupboard for clothing, a rocking chair and a tape deck to go with it. In the end, I had to make do with the fact that I had my own room, a long, dark tunnel with an unfinished paint job and a mattress that sat on wooden crates. At that time it was enough, because Lucia's good mood was like powdered sugar that mercifully covered a not-so-good cake. That good mood continued. For about a year.

Lucia thought that by disrupting Irena's order and system, she would definitively drive her presence out of the flat. But something hidden still lurked.

Lucia didn't know how to clean, didn't know how to take care of basic household- management stuff. She didn't know how to clean up, how and when to air out the place or how to turn off the radiators. In the hottest weather we smothered, breathing air that had been breathed already a million times, and in winter the flat was cold because we didn't let the air out of the radiators. After a year, when the good mood had died, all Lucia did was complain that she was worn out and exhausted again, that she didn't feel like breathing or being awake or even sleeping. The flat was dirty, but it didn't occur to me to clean the toilet and throw away the dried-out mustard that was in the fridge. I cleaned whatever caught my eye, what I tripped over, things that prevented me from entering a room or the bathroom. When there was nothing to put the fish salad onto, I washed the piles of dishes that randomly appeared, even though Lucia almost never cooked. I emptied the garbage when you couldn't even fit a popsicle stick into it without something else falling out. I wiped the floor so that I wouldn't have to wash my socks too often. I knew how to run three programs on the automatic washer and sort the laundry. My classmate Dorota's father taught me that, because Lucia never felt like reading the user's manual.

My classmate Dorota's father was named Peter. Don't call me uncle, he told me. Call me Peter. This wasn't a problem for me, I didn't even call my own mother Mama.

I wanted to have Peter at home, to sit on his knee, listen to him breathing, breathe with him. Put my arm around his neck and eat sandwiches made by him. Sandwiches with mustard. Dorota couldn't stand mustard, but I always wanted mustard because then I could count how many he'd made for me and how many for Dorota. A measurable amount of sympathy.

A tantalizing confidence emanated from him, which was missing in Irena, Lucia and all her friends. Large, grown-up Peter, a man twenty years older than me, who I could touch, who had answers and time for everything and who could teach me how to do laundry.

When an older woman in the bus discreetly whispered that she could smell me and at that moment it dawned on me why no one at school wanted to share a locker with me. Lucia didn't care and I was ashamed to tell Peter. That's why I made up a story that we had a new washing machine and that Lucia had lost the user's manual. We'd had the washing machine for a long time, but Lucia never felt like doing laundry. She would rather wait for some friend and tell him that the washing machine wasn't working and could he have a look at it. This story worked, and so from time to time, someone would do our laundry.

Peter sat me down on the washing machine and spent half an hour teaching me how to read the signs on the clothing labels. He paid full attention to me for half an hour and I had the feeling that I was stepping into the deck of the well-docked boat.

After a year, little by little, everything started to go bad. Lucia's good mood dried up like water from a badly installed tap, drop by drop, together with drops of vodka and absinthe.

While we were living in a sublet, she had to watch herself, but in her own flat, she could do what she wanted.

She often went out and left me alone or with her girl-friends. She would go to work, some work that she couldn't name exactly. In the beginning she tried to pretend that she had a regular decent job somewhere in an office, but I wasn't stupid, and I soon understood that no one works in an office from three-thirty in the afternoon until two in the morning. She realized that I knew she was lying, so she just started coming and going without any explanations and bringing home money. When it wasn't her, it was her friends. When they asked me at school what my mother did, I made something up. She never warned me about her comings and goings and it disturbed me. If I had been a little older then, I guess only her arrivals would have disturbed me. The kids in the housing complex envied me that I was often home alone at night and could watch films. Sometimes Lucia and I didn't even speak to each other for ten days. And I told myself that love doesn't require words. There was some song that went like that.

It took me years to understand how deep relationships have to be, how much love there has to be in those relationships for them not to require words. I was almost thirty and I met Peter again after several decades. Until then I had mostly met people who only shut their traps when they were drinking or smoking. I had adjusted to it, it wasn't hard, sometimes it was enough to smile and say the same thing someone else had said ten minutes earlier. It worked like the child's game 'telephone'—the first one says something in the ear of the second, that one whispers to the third, and that's how everyone receives the message. Some words, any words, they didn't have to make sense, it was a game. The purpose was to make the time you had to spend in the company of others pass.

I had a work CV, the basic facts presented in a table, additional information in parentheses or below the line, nice graphics, elegant language. In folders downloaded from the Internet, wonderfully sterile and average. Anyone could pull an identical piece of paper out of their pocket and present it as the essence of their life, because anyone could go to elementary school on Nobel Street, graduate from high school, get a type-B driver's license and go to the cinema or read books in their free time. When I looked at that piece of paper, I felt like one of the masses. Faceless amongst a million faceless.

Peter didn't want any information from me, not that evening or any other time after that. He didn't ask what I'd done during those years since he'd taught me how to do laundry. It could have seemed like disinterest, but I had the feeling that some healing substances were beginning to flow between the two of us, between two people who, at first glance, didn't seem to suit each other at all.

It was late September, a warm Indian summer, when we sat down at a table on the terrace of a restaurant. The table was set as if for an Italian delegation and I was an unexpected guest for whom the wonderful waiters made room before they realized that I hadn't been included in the original plan. Peter was a little thrown off and took a long time choosing a soup. Dorota rattled on like a cogwheel with a broken tooth. The waiters noiselessly flew around us like comets, spoons, forks and knives clinked, music played, crab claws cracked, the caramel crust of crème brûlée was shattered, the chairs creaked, people stood up and sat down. And between all this movement and us, twilight suddenly began to fall, as quietly and naturally as when it gets dark in the evening. The lights went out, the room went silent, the table shrank, Dorota's cogs got stuck.

At a certain moment Peter touched my hand and it wasn't by chance. It was like a deliberate blast in the glass case at a jewellery shop. Electric eel, I said. Dorota laughed, looking at the filet on my plate.

Electric eel. I said it to him again when we were making love in the vineyard, among the overgrown vines above Raca, about a month later. At that time, almost all the vineyards on the slope were abandoned and neglected. While their owners were trying to officially turn the land into housing lots, the vines grew without supervision or care, the grapes getting smaller every year, acacia-wood posts listing, wires falling on the ground and burrowing into the soil.

We waded through the tall grass, crawled under wires, went from one terrace to the next, terraces of grapevines divided by steep partitions, hills covered with dried-out vine stumps, cherry trees and raspberry bushes. We stopped way up at the top below the wood in the ditch between two rows of vines, we tramped down the grass and put down a blanket. It was noon, the city below us growling like a hungry dog, and I pondered that a few hundred metres to the left was Miletic's garden. The thought was short-lived, a naked sentence which flew through my head like a snowball and fell to pieces. Like when a man meets a woman whom he used to see long ago and cannot even remember her name.

He lay on the blanket, his head between two trampled stalks of mint geranium. At a certain moment he opened his eyes, looked up over my shoulder and said, God, so many birds! From the acacias surrounding the vineyard a whole flock had truly just taken off. The birds circled for a moment above the forest and as suddenly as they had taken off, landed and grew quiet again. Before leaving, Peter put his hand on my breast one more time. Electric eel, I said.

Irena was brought down by illness and weakness faster than her peers, and this undermined her plans and was a real blow to her self-confidence. Other women her age calmly became members of the audience at television shows or roamed the city with tiny steps in search of inexpensive meat. On the tram they pulled up their blouses and showed all of the city the badly healed scars on their flabby bellies. Irena shut herself into the flat, surrendering her whole being to this deceit. She was surprised by this accelerated ageing process, compacted into a few years, and by the pain which in the compacting process had not been reduced. Everything had piled up and she didn't know what had gone wrong. She, who had always known everything. Now, suddenly, she didn't even know her name.

She refused a wheelchair. I think she was worried—and she was right—that then we would stop taking care of her completely because she would be much more mobile and we would think to ourselves, you can manage, do it yourself. But maybe her concerns had something to do with the knowledge that with a wheelchair she would sink another level lower, under the horizon, that she would have to look up at people, look into their nostrils. Perhaps with a wheelchair she would have lived ten more years.

After Irena died, it took me a long time to get used to our empty flat. We had always lived with someone before—in the dormitory, in the back room of a pensioner who couldn't pay her rent, on the couch in Lucia's friend's skincare salon. Now I came home from school and there was no one home. Empty chairs, messy sheets on the bed, on the table a note or even nothing at all. Sometimes I longed for that one endless year when the three of us lived in the flat. When one would go out, the other would always stay behind with me.

Lucia. Call me Lucia. I'm no old cow, Mama repeated. Gradually we began to work as two independent units, Lucia and I.

Even without a mother, I was capable of taking full care of myself and the flat. With Irena I had learnt a lot, especially how to cook. She told me what to buy if I wanted crepes for lunch and then I followed her instructions. I would bring the measuring cups, boxes and pots to her bed and she would say 'good' or 'one more spoonful and then mix'. She never ate anything I gave her, it was enough for her to eat the lunch from the cafeteria and a roll with milk for dinner. She would tear the roll into pieces herself and then pour ultra-pasteurized milk over it.

Sometimes three or four days would go by without Lucia and I seeing each other. I couldn't sit at home and wait for her because she could never tell me when she was coming back, and even if she could, she never kept her word anyway. I preferred to wander around outside in the fresh air and it was then that Lucia would come home, as if on purpose. She would leave money on the table for one or two days, it was only by this that I could guess when she would return, or she would leave food in a plastic bag with a short note, just three words, a lone sentence so that I knew whether she needed something from the pharmacy or the grocer's. She often forgot to take the food out of the bag, forgot or didn't feel like it, and then I had to wipe up melted butter, eat rolls that were stuck together and slice rotten peaches. At home, I could only look around in the half-empty rooms, measure with my steps a place that look like the furniture had been stolen. That sad flat, the place itself was sad.

After Irena's death, along with the flat, we became the owners of a garden. In the inheritance proceedings we found out that after the revolution, Irena had, for incomprehensible reasons, purchased a garden that an emigrant named Miletic had been renting, a property among the old garden plots somewhere above the railway station. In the beginning, Lucia wasn't interested in it, it didn't even occur to her to go see it, check it out, see what condition it was in or revive it.

Soon after Irena's death, the owner of the neighbouring garden plot came to her with a proposal to buy hers.

Lucia was annoyed by these things that came up and didn't even let him into the flat. When, however, he came back a second and third time, the speculator in Lucia awoke and she said to herself that if the neighbour is making such an effort to get this pathetic property, there must be something there. She copied the land registry map, which he had brought with him, gave me some pliers and a ring full of keys that Irena had left behind and sent me to check out the situation.

And even though after a cursory survey of the garden, I didn't find anything that could be turned into money, Lucia said she wouldn't sell it for the world. It was then that I began to live my other life.

The garden hut, garden and abandoned vineyards belonged to a world completely different from the housing complex and the dilapidated stadium with the listless children hiding in the empty locker rooms. It was a green kingdom where I alone ruled, my sovereign territory, pampered, adored. It was my den, a place that offered a previously unknown poetry and peace. Real peace, from within and without. Deep breaths in and out. With each inhalation strength, and each exhalation cleansing. Quiet. Fragrant. Grass taller than I. Images that were disrupted only by cats, rats, weasels and birds and sometimes by homeless people who were on their way from Eastern Slovakia to the metropolis, had got off at the Vineyard Railway Station, and the first thing they came upon were wooden huts in abandoned gardens.

No one had cared for this garden for twenty years. I had never in my life planted something in the ground, but, despite this, the garden was fertile and generous. Over the fence into our garden, the neighbour regularly threw garbage like weeds, strawberry shoots and vine clippings that had set down roots in some ditch and decided to survive. Close to the fence grew a large variety of plants determined to fight with the garden spade, to flower and mature. There one could find currants, blackberries, and dwarfed, stained gooseberry bushes from which the berries always fell before they had ripened. Tulips bloomed, as well as roses and violet columbines and, later in the autumn, georginas. Under the eaves of the roof grape vines and clematis grew, shoots winding around a nail that once held up the rain gutter. Two flattened coins I found on the train tracks hung from the window frame. They were as big as a child's hand and one had a slightly thick and turned- up rim. I made holes in them with a nail, put some twine through them and then watched through the window as they hit each other when the wind blew or clinked and glittered when the sun shone on them.

The electrical wires were kept above the ground only by running them through a divided wooden stick that was lodged in the hollow post of the neighbour's fence. In front of the hut, reared up like a cobra, the water pipe stood sticking up out of the grass.

Inside, I always kept it clean, I regularly swept the linoleum floor and shook out the blankets in front of the hut. The hut held a bed, chair and two shelves. One was full of toys, and on the other were pots, a wooden spoon and cutlery and—like an exhibit of period porcelain—cups and glasses remaining from various collections that sparkled. Over the holes in the plastic drywall I pasted posters, covering the wounds with tape or pieces of wood. Behind the door, propped up against the wall, stood an unloaded air rifle for scaring away annoying little boys who crawled around on the other side of the fence and tried wherever they could to steal things. In the corner was a three-legged cast-iron stove, a mysterious thing whose function long escaped me. Until a few handfuls of ash came out of it. On the stove was a heavy torch, a rusty knife, some matches and several glass candle lanterns. All of these things were supposed to protect me from perverts, drunk and hungry homeless people, thieves, tramps, Boogeymen and roving sheep-slaughterers. Because the sun didn't always shine or the birds chirp. Sometimes when I was in the garden it rained, or was dark and the wind whistled outside and the trees creaked, unripe apples feel onto the tin roof, mice rustled under the drywall and I was, after all, a housing-complex child, a child used to hearing the water running down through the pipes from floor to floor at worst.

At some point, Miletic had come by a huge quantity of blue paint and, thus, everything that needed to be painted over a number of years was painted blue. The blue hut with white shutters looked like a steamboat lost in the grass. It was blue on the inside, a blue chair and bed too, the fence had been blue and the stones that formed the path as well. The path became overgrown with grass, but was washed by the rain, and sky-blue stones now lay about in the hollows throughout the garden. I could have sworn that they moved around, all by themselves, pushed by a mysterious, supernatural force. Because no earthly being could have had a reason to roll them around. It was my little garden mystery.

In contrast to the amiability of my garden, every time I returned home, there stood before me my five-story concrete building with no lift, sewn together like a blanket of grey squares, with the windows blinking in uniform rhythm. Some balconies were glassed in, some wrapped in plastic or corrugated metal, hung with geraniums and wet carpets, from which water ran down onto the geraniums. It was already clear from a distance that in these boxes everyone just lived their own lives and with those around them no one cooperated, fought nor united.

The way home from the garden to the housing complex took me about fifteen or twenty minutes. The whole way I was thinking about the dead cat that I had just buried, but it was enough to see our building and that poor cat stopped meowing in my head.

When I got to the front entrance, I could hear only a few small sounds, a TV ad, a dog barking, a mixer running and a loud conversation, which I tried to understand. It could have been about eight o'clock and the TV series about hospitals was starting. Through an open window a cork popped and something splashed into a glass. With hands in my pockets, I leant against the door with all my weight—like all children in the world who do simple things in a complicated way— and as the heavy door gave way, I realized that I had been completely alone outside. There weren't any children playing anywhere anymore, even the band of boys from the next entrance had gone in, the ones who hung out after sundown and during school. I was the last one and totally alone. No one was accompanying me, I hadn't parted with anyone, I hadn't exchanged a word with anyone the whole day. It reminded me of a time from First Grade when the whole class went on a field trip to the water amusement park and I was the only one whose mother said that you can bathe just as easily in a bathtub.

You could actually find the positive in my situation. After all, how many kids beg to be able to stay out at least until eight, crying, yelling, having to take out the garbage, washing the steps or bringing Daddy beer from the night grocers. To the amusement of others, full of shame, but determined to come to a stalemate with their parents at least in one small war. They have to negotiate and extort because they know very well the effect it has on tired parents—they have a sense of how much their parents can take.

And I, alone in the dark garden, behind a hedge, above the pulsing city, I had got it all as a gift and didn't have to do anything, anything at all. Was it good then? Or bad? Where were all the kids that evening, the ones who were always outside for days at a time? What did their parents do and what did they do when the apartment door closed behind them, at eight o'clock, in August, in the middle of the city? How did they spend the last days of their summer holidays? Did they too sit in front of the television? Suffering every night in front of some film that their parents generously let them watch—because you were good today—that they didn't understand and that continued even in their dreams when they lay curled up in their little beds trying to think of something nice? Did it sometimes happen that they were forced to stay out in the hall an hour or two while Lucia did something that couldn't be put off, for which she needed an empty flat? And what about the parents? Did they sigh in relief when they finished chasing the untiring child with toothbrush in hand around the flat and that child finally went into his room and stopped bothering them with demands for attention? Parents, who were tired from work, from the heat, from their entire long lives that they had to live, from the repeated daily rituals that are good for their children but that exhaust them? When night after night they into an armchair instead of being able to do what they really want? Do they even remember what they like to do?

Or do they just mechanically repeat what they did yesterday and the day before and the year before? Or do they wonder how great it would be if they could spend one or two more hours with the children and look forward to them crawling into their bed at six in the morning?

In the building opposite ours, on the second floor, lived seven-year-old Christian. He was always clean, hair combed and well-dressed, because his aunt sent him clothes from London. He always had everything in his school bag, knew how to greet people properly and, even though he wasn't blessed with excess intelligence, he tried hard and did fairly well in school. The kids at school liked him because he wasn't annoying. Then, suddenly, he started to push pins under his fingernails. His mother took him to the school psychologist and then the poor thing suffered more because the whole school made fun of him, calling him an idiot and a retard, even more than they did when he didn't know how to hold a pencil properly.

What was he doing that evening after sundown? It was August, still warm and nice outside. He was looking for a quiet corner in their big, four-room flat, where he didn't have his own bedroom, because his mother wanted to receive guests in a separate room, which she called a salon, and his father had another room as his office? Did he sit in his father's office under the table trying not to touch his father's legs and make him nervous, did he hide in the darkest corner where he was allowed to sit and imagine how it would be if he could shut himself up in his own room and turn out the light for a little while? To turn on the torch, put his hand on the hot bulb and see his fingers, his red, damaged nails, glowing? To observe the shadows on the wall or just read the letters in the cone of light? Or was he already lying in bed with his mama, because Mama's bed was his bed and her sleep his sleep too? His mama's rhythm was also his body's rhythm because he had nowhere to hide from her love and care. Her breath was his breath, there was no other oxygen in their flat.

What worried Christian's mama most was that she couldn't figure out where he got the new pins. Where had he hidden them when he didn't have his own room or even his own cup-board with a key where he could stow his treasures like all the other children? How could he always outmanoeuvre her when all she did all day was clean their flat, when she knew every movement of their velvet drapes and every gap in the parquet floors? How could he hide in that flat a matchbox full of pins stolen from school bulletin boards, a dried-up beetle and a shiny chip taken from a calculator which he once got in a trade in exchange for his T-shirt from London? She asked us several times, classmates and friends from the complex, whether we knew something about his pins, where he kept his secret stash. She asked each one of us with tears in her eyes to be nice to him and not bother him so that he wouldn't have any reason to hurt his little body.

While I was standing by the front door turning the door handle, was Christian lying in bed? Was he lying in bed with his fingers in his mama's hair because he couldn't fall asleep any other way? Or was he pretending to sleep because in reality he couldn't fall asleep with his mother's raspy breathing, but he couldn't tell her—Mama, I don't need you anymore. I can fall asleep by myself. And when his mama fell asleep first, he pushed his fingers carefully into the slit in the mattress and pulled out the matchbox.

When we were walking home from school together, he told me his big secret. His eyes were shiny with excitement. The sleeves of his sweater were stretched and hung down almost to his knees. In a whisper I advised him to cut the mattress just under the seam and stick the box in between the springs. I told him to do it because I knew that sometimes opening the valves could help you keep your equilibrium.

Two floors above us lived Maya. Two or three times a week she would go fishing with her father. She got up at four-thirty and by five she was already sitting in a folding chair by the gravel-pit lake, looking at the still, dark surface of the water. It was still dark, and Maya was afraid of the dark. She was afraid of deep water, she had lots of fears. Her father lay in a sleeping bag next to her, drunk as a skunk at dawn, a father who wanted a son. He had really wanted to have a son, a big boy with red hair and scraped knees, a boy he could buy a fishing rod.

Then Maya started falling asleep during class. She was as quiet as a fish and stank of them. No one wanted to sit near her, and when she forgot her gym clothes, no one wanted to lend her theirs. When her father or someone who hadn't been fast enough to get drunk by the lake dropped her off at school, she would go into the bathroom, change out of her camouflage pants, put on her pink T-shirt that her mother secretly packed in a non-transparent bag, spray herself with cologne and put on make-up. After school she would go back to the bathroom, wash her face and put her camouflage pants back on. Her father was already home, and the fish were home, circling in the bucket of water, waiting for the long, thin knife that Maya would use to open and gut them. Her father would then brag that his daughter could stick her whole hand into a cut fish and pull out its guts without tearing the skin.

At that time, in the next entrance over, on the same floor, on the other side of the wall from Maya, lived Pete and Mat, twins about eight years old. If they weren't locked in the flat, they were out in the evenings going round the neighbourhood pubs and beer stands looking for their parents. The boys would drag their parents home like dogs, one buried in Mama's coat, the other in Daddy's jacket—two small, weak, undernourished, but unconditionally loving dogs. They were supposed to be in Second Grade with Christian, but their Mama forgot to register them that year, so they were a year behind. Everyone referred to them as the two who had failed First Grade.

How many times did I see them climbing into Maya's bedroom, in their slippers, because their mama had locked up their shoes to keep them from following her? How many times did their feet slip on the metal windowsill and they grabbed the lightning rod at the last minute?

Sometimes, when the wind blew and it was hard to see them among the swaying shadows of the trees, I thought I saw them falling, flying past the windows and hitting the asphalt. First one, because his foot had slipped. Then the other, because he had let go of the drainpipe. They were so little that they wouldn't even leave a crack in the pavement. But at least there were two of them. Twins. Together they were strong. Did they know what loneliness was if they were always together? Did they call each other by name like my Mama and Grandma and me, or did they say my brother, my twin?

The bolt was thrown on the front door so that the door wouldn't shut by itself, it was enough to lean on it and run up the stairs to the third floor, run fast, take the steps two by two, so that no monsters would emerge from the terrifying cellar-darkness, monsters that scare even big kids, school kids who haven't believed in the Bogeyman for years but they just can't forget about him. In the evening they tear up the stairs, buttocks clenched in fear, so that they can unlock their front door or ring the bell for Mama before the automatic light in the stairwell goes off, so that they don't have to live through those terrifying seconds in the darkness and stench of the long hallway feeling along the wall with their hands, breathlessly searching for the light switch. All this just to arrive at the door and find that they don't know which pocket of their bag they've got the keys in, or, as with me, to find to their great disappointment that the lock is blocked from the inside by another key. In our house it was a daily occurrence, but it still always got me down.

As I was trying to push my key deeper into the lock and push Lucia's out from the other side, the light in the hall clicked and went out and the key, teetering in the lock on only one of its teeth, fell out onto the ground. The key fell onto the ground and I was defeated. First, I would feel around the floor in the dark, but when above me on the next floor someone opened a door and shuffled out into the hallway, I quickly stood up and found the switch from memory. I sat down on Irena's night table and began to very slowly untie the shoelaces on my black and white Chinese-made shoes.

Two people were moving down from the floor above. I listened to the sinister approach of shuffling shoes, or rather slippers. Think of something good, I said to myself. Instead, the black cat just started meowing again in my head. He looked like the dusty fur slippers that were carrying the four-legged monster from the fifth floor down the stairs. The steps got closer and I could already see the hands holding the railing, the thin, weak hands of the neighbour. The older alcoholic and his trembling wife, who always kept two paces behind him, like cyclists, one drafting the other to save their strength for another painful move.

While the neighbours' slippers moved forward another centimetre, the light went out again. My fear replaced my anger at Lucia. If she left me a message on the refrigerator or called me in the morning while I was still at home and sacrificed those miserable three crowns, I could wait in the garden, in front of the night grocer's or ride around the city on the tram. This way I couldn't avoid another embarrassing meeting with the neighbours in the narrow hall with the shaky night tables and a scene with tangled shoelaces. The scene that was useless anyway, because the neighbours knew that I couldn't get in the door.

They were embarrassed both for me and themselves. They were both on a disability pension and sat at home all day smoking and drinking by the open window, and when they felt like it, they set out for the street, walked around the complex, he in front, she two paces behind him, clutching in her hand a handbag for balance. They walked to the night grocer's where they bought a flask of alcohol. Sometimes they argued in whispers, this rupture visible only in their tense faces, in the livelier movements of their limbs and heads. The wife's purse bounced around clumsily as she tried to catch up with the husband, keep up with him and walk lightly and straight as she once did when she was still going to work and was capable of making decisions for herself and others. The husband looked like an old, sick animal, and had small, watery eyes, large flapping nostrils searched for available ethanol and his long arms bumped against his thighs. I saw in her some effort to preserve at least a bit of her appearance and style. She went out with make-up on and bought herself colourful suits that got caught on the bushes and were destroyed during her night-time pilgrimages.

I took advantage of the darkness, and while the neighbour was looking for the light switch, I ran past them on the landing so carefully that the two of them felt nothing but a slight current of air by their right arms. I sat down on the last step and rested my head on my knees. Even before the neighbours had shuffled their feet down the last step and the man had put his hand on the handle of the front door, I had already had a short nap.

When I awoke, I was disoriented and tired. It was dark again in the hall and there was cold air coming through the broken window. Beyond the missing windowpane, the hope took shape that this loneliness deep as a well would be filled by at least one small person walking across the street or diagonally across the yard between the buildings, on the grass glistening wet in the night. In one of the windows opposite something moved, but it was just a shadow. Three lights in three flats went out at the same time like a signal. I said to myself that if any three windows light up at the same time again, that I would go downstairs and bang really hard on the door. But before that happened, the door on the third floor opened quickly and someone ran down the stairs without turning on the light. By memory, without tripping. It was someone who came to our house very often. I heard Lucia putting the chain on the door.

Jarka? She said quietly, with a question mark. Lucia, short, hunched up and so thin that she could be pulled through the crack. Come inside, she whispered, she opened the door and a bluish light filled the hall, a light completely different from the hall light. Come in already my dear, she said, as if she were the one waiting for me and not the other way around. Take off your shoes, she didn't forget to point out. Schlapo left something for you, she whispered later in the kitchen with a slightly apologetic smile.

So it was Schlapo. At that time, he came to our house often—every other day, and often stayed the night. It lasted about three months and then, like a clean cut, he never showed up again. After him, someone else simply began to come regularly, as if they had changed the postman. First, they wouldn't know where to go and would knock on someone else's door by mistake, after three weeks, they would be running up in the dark.

On the table were some stickers with pictures of animals that had stopped being interesting to me long ago, but I knew that it would be better to swallow my disappointment. So I thanked her. Please tell Schlapo too, I said. I was really offended, after all I wasn't a child anymore. What was I supposed to do with these stupid stickers? Stick them on my pencil case? So that someone could whack me on the head with it at school?

I felt I'd like to drink something warm—milk, cocoa, tea, something that would warm me up inside, a warm mug that I could rest on my stomach and cup in my hands. On the daily menu, however, were two cold yogurts and so I satisfied myself with that.

How's it going? asked Lucia. Fine, I said. Simple conversation. Thrifty. We didn't look at each other once. Lucia sat on the table, tossing a lighter around in her hands. I stood, leaning against the counter, eating yogurt. That's good, said

Lucia. Or something like that, neutral. Eat the other one too, I'll buy more in the morning. The lighter fell. What did you do today? She asked as she leant down, barely audible. Nothing, I answered. This dialogue had no steam on either side and, thus, crept forward very slowly. I hesitated about whether to mention the cat. I could tell Lucia about it, maybe she'd be interested and she'd listen to me. That I had buried it myself, that I didn't just leave it lying there in the dust, in the sun. That I'm not as self-centred, careless and unfeeling as she says I am.

I found a dead cat, I said, my mouth covered in white yogurt. Where? In front of the garden. You were there again? Why don't you play here in the complex? She stood up, turned on the tap and drank from her hand. She was the same height as me and so standing next to each other we truly looked like sisters. I'm tired, she said then in a different tone, as if she'd completely forgotten about the cat, the garden and the conversation we'd begun, and mechanically stroked my head. As if I were little, like a small child. I threw the yogurt container into the garbage and hopped on one leg into my room.

My room was long and narrow and felt very cramped, because the light from the small window didn't light it completely. It had looked like a normal girl's room, pink walls, pillows, knick-knacks on strings, talismans. Then I took almost all my toys and posters to the garden hut, some things were stolen by Lucia's friends for their various children strewn around the town and some things were destroyed. Lucia liked the empty room enormously and praised me that it was so clean and that nothing was lying around collecting dust. On the walls remained only two lonely newspaper clippings and shiny squares of tape.

I took off my pants and threw them on the chair, knocking over a jar full of pencils. The pencils made a racket, and there was nothing in the room to dampen it. I remained still for a moment, looking at the door, waiting for Lucia to come and say her usual—don't make any trouble, I'm tired.

When I was younger, Lucia thought I wouldn't understand the word 'trouble', so instead she would say, be good or I won't love you. Anyone can understand that. Being good and loving someone. So I tried with all my might to be good. When I did something wrong, I was afraid that Lucia would abandon me, that she wouldn't come back from one of her night walks. I imagined myself standing by the window waiting for Lucia, standing by the window for several days, hungry and having peed in my pants, but not daring to leave the window. Because if I left the window, I would miss the moment when Lucia came back, and I wouldn't be able to keep her there if, by the front entrance, she suddenly changed her mind. It could happen any time and I sometimes felt real, paralysing fear that I would do something bad and it would be a problem and I wouldn't even realize it. That night I didn't have to be afraid because Lucia had already fallen asleep and once she had fallen asleep, she would sleep like a log. I washed my face and crawled into bed.

I had a dream. I was walking around an abandoned swimming pool. Yellowed, curled-up leaves were flying around in the breeze and dropping onto the surface. They swam like ducks, bobbing and spinning around on their axis. The swimming area was empty, it was the end of summer, maybe even September, and all the children were at school. The water was dirty. On the opposite side of the pool, far from me, in a little, blue wooden boat, in a square cabin that looked very much like the garden hut, sat Peter. Peter was loudly urging me not to be afraid and jump in the water, but I was afraid and cold. Peter came out of the cabin. He balanced in the doorway, waving some unsold pool-admission tickets at me and shouted, go underwater Jarka, you'll feel better underwater, go under Jarka, swim! Swim to me! His eyes were shining, smiling.

I swam. With my head underwater, with a deep breath and eyes closed, not thinking about the depth of the pool and the garbage that was hitting my shoulders and interrupting the rhythm of my strokes. There was a moment when I saw myself from above, from the viewpoint of the flying leaves, I watched myself moving my arms and legs in a regular, rhythmic motion, my head smoothly moving through the water, my hair flowing. Reflections from the waning sun and two strong spotlights hit the surface of the water deforming the shape of my body. Like when you look at the world through a full glass of water. Through a bottle, through water. I saw Peter throwing the tickets into the water, a full handful of little white papers, like confetti at a party.

I swam to him, the whole length of the pool in one breath, because at that moment I didn't need anyone else. One strong adult, who would listen to me without conditions and give me answers to all my questions.

I swam and my hair detached from my scalp. First one or two thin strands, then with each stroke more and more, I left them behind me like water reeds, waving in the water with regular movements.

I came up for air. The pool was full of hair, but the hair on my head was still there. The boat had disappeared, Peter had disappeared and in his place were only the small pieces of paper which stuck to my body.

The next morning, I woke up unbearably hungry. The refrigerator, however, was empty. After the two yogurts I had eaten the evening before, there remained only the sad spaces between several empty compote jars. At first glance it was clear that Lucia had not yet been to the shops and the money on the table meant that she wasn't going either. I didn't even have to read the brief message written on a cigarette paper. Grocery shopping. She could have written more.

If she had used her mind, if she had chosen to use smaller letters, she could have written even ten words on that thin, almost transparent piece of paper. Except that she never made anything complicated. She never took any extra trouble. Jarka, just no unnecessary trouble, OK? That was her mantra, her recipe for a peaceful life. Before that she used to draw me a smiley face, or something like that, which got spilt on and distorted in a drop of water. Then I couldn't remember whether I was supposed to do something . . . I was always supposed to do something. The laundry, the garbage, homework.

My hunger was getting unpleasant and my stomach started to hurt. I took everything that resembled food out of the refrigerator and cupboards and lined it up on the kitchen table. I wouldn't throw dried-out mustard, baking powder, two damp teabags and a cub of beef bouillon into a pot together even if I were cooking glue. I went through the entire flat, but besides an unfinished piece of bread and butter left on a greasy piece of paper by the bed in Lucia's room, I didn't find anything else to eat.

It was seven-thirty. I calculated that if I got dressed very slowly, brushed my teeth really thoroughly and walked normally, not skipping, I would get to the local grocer's after it had opened for the day. Then I wouldn't have to stand in front of the big glass doors with the light censor and watch the ladies loading the fresh rolls into the bin.

I put on the same clothes I'd been wearing the day before and opened the clothes closet just to kill some time. The closet was half-empty. In the sock drawer there was one lonely pair balled up, some jeans, two T-shirts and no clean underwear. I looked at myself in the mirror in the hallway. My shorts were dirty from two weeks of constant wear, but when I wiped them a bit with a wet rag, they were good for another week. The T-shirt was OK, I took good care of it. I'd worn it for three days and slept in it twice to air the second-hand stink out of it. And so that the small green flowers that were on it would take on my own scent. You couldn't even close the laundry basket, two-thirds of my closet and some men's T-shirts were hanging out of it. Another week had gone by without the laundry being done, as Lucia would say, because for Lucia, things were done by themselves, shopping was done, some-thing was scratched, things got fixed, things got washed, tomorrow, on Thursday, in a month.

On the way across the complex, diagonally, along the scratchy, yellowed, trampled-down grass path, I met a group of boys of various ages. The youngest was seven, Christian from the building opposite, and the oldest I guessed to be fifteen, although I didn't know him well. He wasn't from our part of the complex. He was trying really hard to control the expression on his face, attempting to look grown-up and defi-ant, taking big steps and holding a cigarette between his thumb and forefinger such that it was going to burn his fingers any minute. He didn't have it quite down yet.

The boys were all different but moved around like puppies from the same litter. They tried to equalize themselves so that one didn't have more or less and no one was worse or better off than the others. They slumped, they spat thick, slimy mucus and jammed their hands down into their pockets as far as they could go. When they went by a glass shop window, they surreptitiously checked out their reflection and then slumped more and picked up their feet even less.

Hey Jarka! The tallest one called to me and tipped his cap so I could see the badly disguised interest in his eyes. Got a cig? He asked. I stopped but hid the plastic bag behind my back. I don't, I said carelessly. Carelessly, because I didn't have to pretend in front of them. They didn't interest me, definitely not as much as they interested Dorota, who talked of nothing else than who looked at her when and whether they spit under her feet. Because it already meant something. It was almost like physical contact. The girls were always looking for someone and then they just happened to walk by his building or started to be friendly with his sister. These boys didn't impress me, I knew they were weak, that they cried. And when they were older, they'd cry too.

When they asked me to, I went with them, had fun with them, ran with them from basement to basement, sat next to them on the dilapidated stadium grandstand. I smoked when they offered, but I wouldn't bring them Lucia's cigarettes. I didn't feel connected to them—we had no common secrets. I was bored and so I took what came. If I could spend my day the way I wanted, I would sit down in Peter's kitchen, send Dorota out to be with the boys, and watch Peter make lunch. And then I would sit next to him and eat that hot lunch. I would wish him bon appétit and he would look into my eyes. That would truly be enough for me. You are totally weird, Dorota said to me when I confided my thoughts to her. For her, Peter's lunch, conversation and table covered with a clean tablecloth were a daily given.

You're a cow, the boys said to me on a regular basis. They were mean to me, they chased me around the complex and took my stuff, but then they always came to me afterwards, waited for me in front of the entrance, gave me half their baguette. They did it quietly, so that I didn't see all the stuff behind it. They used the fact that I often had money on me, on the other hand, they were envious of my freedom, because I could be out even after ten, while by eight they were sitting in front of the door shining shoes and spitting chewed-up evergreen needles into the pot of geraniums so they wouldn't smell like cigarettes and herb liquor. They were jealous that I was often at home alone, watched films that they couldn't and had the whole flat to myself. Lucia brought me nice clothes from her travels and clothes were always important. I lived their unfulfilled dreams every day. And I didn't care. Retards.

Come with us to the grandstand, I'll show you something, said the oldest—that is, Pete. But we're supposed to call him Pepo, whispered Christian to me, and without waiting for the opinions or agreement of the others, he walked away in the direction of the stadium. I'm hungry, I said. I didn't slip and say that I was heading to the shops, but the boys had already caught the scent of money. Christian is sure to have something, don't you Christian? He nodded his head at the seven-year-old boy with the enormous, frightened eyes and the small backpack. Christian was one of the smallest kids—he was entering Second Grade— a little tyke who always hopped up and down around the big boys like a bunny ready to serve and learn. Christian always carried a mid-morning snack with him, said the group and laughed. Everyone envied him those beautifully wrapped, fragrant snacks, but they were chicken, and not one of them would admit it.

That day I got the snack instead, and in the beginning, no one knew why I deserved it, no one knew what thing Pepo had planned to get in return. It worked. Christian and I were at the end of the procession, Christian skipping so that he wouldn't fall too much behind, he pulled from his backpack the sought-after wrapped-up sandwich and a granola bar—a surprise from Mama. Another one that he'd saved from the previous day was hidden in his trouser pocket. He unintentionally revealed this to me, but his granola bars didn't interest me. Bread was good enough.

We crawled through a hole in the fence, ran across the grass pretending to be a field with its barely visible white lines, squeezed through a door hanging crooked on one hinge and, revelling in the illegality and feeling of brotherhood and security in numbers, we made it over mountains of garbage, ripped-out car seats and crushed bricks. We sat down on the top row, where there was a good view of part of the chemical factory and the field—the white lines now emerging from the grass like a message written in invisible ink or milk lit from below by a candle. Under the bench they had hidden a bong and in the garbage bin under the stairs they had an open bottle of homemade wine. They offered some to me first, and I drank, I didn't even hesitate, a whole decilitre in one breath without coughing, and I knew that I had risen a level in their eyes again. The alcohol wasn't strong, it had a sourish, some-what-stale taste. It was definitely something I didn't want to repeat, but the slight but lingering tipsiness was nice.

After me everyone took a drink in turns, even the smallest wet their lips. They were afraid that if they refused out of disgust they'd be ridiculed, and they knew it was repulsive, just like everything they had ever tasted under similar circum-stances, and that they would have to try their damnedest not to throw up because that would be the end.

Then someone did pull out some cigarettes after all and, with great hesitation, offered them to the others. Don't you have any others? Maybe tomorrow. But we have to get some you-know-what. Weed. One said it and he said it very slowly emphasizing each sound, so that everyone would realize what he was talking about, so that everyone would read between the lines, because at that moment it was a big thing—a couple of marijuana plants grown in the jungle of underbrush by one of the Danube tributaries, or in the cupboard under neon lights.

So, I laid into the sandwich again. Two paper-thin, light slices glued together with egg-salad. Little Christian looked on with sorrow as his mid-morning snack irretrievably disappeared into my mouth, but he pretended to look happy because he had served me, a kindred spirit, a big, serious girl who everyone knew roamed the complex after dark and didn't wear one of those awful, hard-as-a-rock padded bras, but under whose shirt you could see two mounds that jiggled when she walked, like Mama's pudding. He looked me over from bottom to top, tennis shoes, scratched calves, knees pressed together, T-shirt, hands smeared with egg spread, sunken cheeks and hair carelessly swept up in an elastic band high on the crown of my head. He must have seen that the plastic bag I'd put down next to me had been taken behind the seat by someone who was going through it. There was loud howling from the others, who had already understood why Christian had had to sacrifice his snack. The howling was meant to distract me. Christian could see very well what was happening, but he couldn't do anything—at that moment he couldn't decode the connection between the sudden improvement in the older boys' mood, the fallen plastic bag and his chewed-up sandwich. I saw helplessness in his cute little face, but I thought he was just grieving for his snack. So as not to be completely overwhelmed by his confusion, he began to show off like the rest, jumping up onto the bench and howling with them, unconvinced and hesitant.

It was then that I began to wonder what I was actually doing there. Why did I always let myself be enticed by such idiots who jumped up and down around me like monkeys and shouted in my ear? Why didn't I just tell them to screw off and let me keep walking? I would rather be bored and hungry than spend time with those morons. If I at least liked one of them, but I couldn't even say that. Little Christian, I said to myself, if his mother manages, if she doesn't suffocate him completely, he may grow up into a handsome and complex being, but with the others it was clear. They'd get through vocational school, get their classmates pregnant and drink the rest of their lives away. Or they'd go off to work in Ireland and then do the same when they got back. The only difference would be that they wouldn't be squeezed into a flat with their parents and their children, because they'd buy a studio for that Irish money. Where would I be then, I wondered.

This embarrassing comedy was ended by big boss Pepo, who suddenly jumped up onto the bench, threw down his unfinished cigarette, came up behind me and grabbed me firmly by the breasts with both hands.

Retard!!! I screamed with my mouth full of crumbs and little squares of chopped egg exploding into the air. Pepo continued to laugh idiotically jumping from bench to bench, he jumped up and down at the bellowing laughter of the others and stuck the middle finger of one hand into a circle formed by the thumb and forefinger of the other.

I felt sick, like those times when the big sweaty hand of the Engineer landed on my breast.

At home I didn't scream or complain, I just quietly suffered through those few minutes, because it always took only a couple of minutes, as long as it took to go down the stairs from the third floor, smoke one cigarette outside in the fresh air and come back up, but that's not what he did. He told Lucia that he was going for a smoke, that he liked to smoke outside in the fresh air, he would put on his shoes, slam the door and then tiptoe into my room. I didn't want to make trouble, so I was quiet. It didn't happen often, once or twice a month, when he had the chance, maybe more often, maybe also when I was deeply asleep, I don't know. He didn't do anything more than that, just held onto my breast, belly or down there. He didn't want me to do anything except lie there quietly and put two or three fingers into his mouth. It didn't hurt, I didn't feel anything while he was doing it, sometimes I just felt sick to my stomach from the heat and stench under the covers. Sometimes I felt ridiculous, sometimes I was afraid. But less and less with time. I learnt how to switch off the fuses and cut the connection with the world. Sometimes I even thought that it was normal, because no one ever told me that it wasn't.

It seemed to me then that this idiot had humiliated me a hundred times more. He'd humiliated me in front of the others, outside.

At that moment I saw boys, faces twisted with laughter, a confused Christian hugging his backpack to his little tyke chest, flashes of light refracting through a bottle flying through the air. I didn't hear any sounds, like laughter, the stamping of tennis shoes on the benches or falling plastic bottles bursting on the concrete. For a moment all my fuses went out.

Then suddenly, as if someone had thrown a switch, the sound came back on and my ears filled with laughter. I shook myself, threw away the rest of the sandwich—Christian watched its trajectory and inglorious end in the gap between two crushed bricks—grabbed a piece of wood ripped from a bench and hurled it with all my strength, surprised at how much force I had in me from the anger. Pepo bled, a crooked nail in the wood had torn his earlobe.

While he was putting himself back together, recovering and realizing what had happened, while he was exchanging his mask of self-confidence for the face of a horrified, stuttering child, I managed to jump over the benches and down the steps, run across the lawn and run down the path between the buildings onto the main road. I jumped onto a departing bus and rode one stop. My heart was beating like a bell, high, like it did sometimes when I heard it in my sleep.

Retard. Idiot. Asshole. Prick. I quietly said all the curses I had heard at home over and over. Bastard. Shit. Imbecile. Limpdick. Pervert. Fucker. Dumbass. Pathetic fool. I imagined him sitting there among the garbage, with his hair gummed up with blood, alone, because his buddies had got scared and run off. I knew he wasn't dead, because even though I had aimed at his head, not counting on the nail sticking out, I hadn't intended to kill him or permanently damage his facade. I could have hit him a hundred times more, I could have kicked. And then hit him again. And again. But I didn't do it. What for?

It wasn't until I was standing at the checkout counter with a full basket of groceries in my hand that I found they had pinched all my money. The saleswoman knew me and, with a merciful and worried smile took the wafer cookies, butter and ham and left me with three rolls. I stuffed them in my face one after the other, leaving the third for later. I thought about how I definitely still had some compote or a can of tuna in the garden hut. I actually looked forward to school, because at school I had meal tickets and at least once a day could count on a real meal.

The road to the vineyards and gardens wound among houses with small gardens, along the tram tracks, across the cross-walks for pedestrians at the traffic lights, past the railway station and under the railway bridge. In front of the station stood a newsstand with magazine covers glued all over its walls. In my hands I firmly clutched the bag with one roll in it, browsed the magazine covers and dreamt about arriving at the garden hut, and eating the roll with some jam that I definitely had stashed somewhere on a shelf. The magazine covers were faded and wrinkled, one covered part of the other and the headlines melded into meaningless sentences. Between two rows of magazines the penetrating eyes of the saleswoman peered out at me, she was convinced that I wanted to steal something. She looks like the type, she was definitely saying to herself, moving the miniature window down such that all you could stick through the space was one rolled-up magazine. Through this narrow gap I looked into her eyes and saw Irena in them, something that I certainly didn't need for a happy life.

I chose rather to go up a steep staircase into the railway station's long, defaced hall that was covered from floor to ceiling with graffiti. Above the entrance was a broken security camera with yanked-out cables sticking out of the wall, and the door to the bathroom, which I wanted to use, was locked. Up some more stairs I came out onto the platform and sat down on a bench.

At that moment I remembered the little piece of paper I'd seen on Lucia's night table under the dried-out piece of bread. On the paper were train-departure times written in Lucia's handwriting and her face appeared before my eyes, fuzzy and distorted like a reflection in the window of a departing train. Maybe she was only going somewhere nearby, to St George's or Modra, maybe I would see her here, I hoped so. I would see her getting off or on a train, or just see her face in the window, at that moment I didn't care which. I just needed to know where she was and whether she was all right. Since I had had such a messed-up morning, she could have been having a similar one. I wished for it to be so, so that the connection between us wouldn't be broken.

I imagined us sitting together on a train, leg to leg, chatting. We are sitting next to each other and going, for example, on an outing. To Red Castle or for a swim at the lake—it was still warm, we could still do it. I put my head on Lucia's shoulder, our hair mingling. On my knees is an unfinished piece of cake. Lucia is dozing and murmuring on and off. Two, three words, pause, short dream, two, three words, pause, inhale. The wheels of the train rhythmically click-clack to Lucia's melodious humming and there is something magical and soothing in these sounds, like a good weather forecast for the coming days.

Instead, two cargo trains rushed around me, with such a deafening rumble that I had to cover my ears and close my eyes. A strange smell lingered in the air over the rails and moved the muscles in the faces of the tired people a little. Lucia did not get off any of the three commuter trains or the one express train, nor did I see her on the platform or at the station buffet. Down in the waiting room, I had almost approached a girl who looked like Lucia her from the back, but the girl turned around in time for me to see that she was not.

I went back onto the street where the newsstand was. The tin hut was locked, the grate drawn down over the window and there was a note stuck to it from the inside saying that the old hag would be right back. I looked over the other side of the stand thoroughly as well. I didn't feel like leaving, wasn't in a hurry to go anywhere and nothing was pressing me to move. Lucia might arrive on the next train, or any train. I was sorry I hadn't looked at that piece of paper with the numbers more closely and taken it with me. I told myself that I'd leave when the woman came back to the stand and pulled up the grate.

Lucia didn't teach me to do laundry, but she did teach me a very useful game. A game for the weak. I find anything that moves from point A to point B, something I can count, something with a beginning and an end. More or less predictable or regular. I set the boundary, goal, the endpoint, and wait. When I don't know how long to let the soup cook, I wait until three crows fly by the window. If I don't know whether to turn right or left, I wait until I hear a dog barking from one side or other. I'm afraid to leave too early when I'm waiting for something, but what if I'm already feeling impatient? Then I leave when the neighbour on the bench finishes his cigarette or puts down his newspaper. You don't have to take responsibility for both the small and big decisions always and everywhere, you can let it go and just watch, Lucia said. It's nice not to think too much. It's easy to let yourself be led by chance, to copy the direction of the wind, the path of a flying piece of paper or a stray dog.

The woman from the newsstand wasn't coming back and I heard a faint sobbing, and an insistent 'sssssss' sound. Under the stairs a woman was moving from one side to the other of a large pram made for twins. On one side slept a small child— perhaps five or ten months old, I couldn't quite tell, and next to it there was a totally identical child crying. The crying child could wake up the sleeping one, so the woman was trying to calm it down. She was short and round, dressed in a loose cotton T-shirt that was sticking to her and unnecessarily emphasizing her slack body. She was dishevelled and clumsy, constantly running into the carriage wheels with the tips of her sandals and moved things around—rattles and diapers— from one hand to the other. When she had calmed the child down, she looked around, terrified, to see if there was anyone nearby who was disturbed or annoyed by the crying. She smiled at me, the apologetic smile of someone embarrassed to accept help or a gift. The smile of mothers whose own children curse vulgarly or throw themselves down onto the pavement in a tantrum.

There was no one else standing on the pavement in front of the station, the little square was empty and there was no one to feel ashamed in front of. The woman rocked the carriage a bit, and when she had ensured that both children were breathing regularly, she looked at the entrance to the station with its twenty-two steep steps and then back at the carriage as big as an aircraft carrier. With bent arms she made a gesture of despair and helplessness. Apparently, she wanted to go up onto the platform, right to the train that was just then being announced, but she couldn't get that carriage up there by herself. A voice with comically clear pronunciation was already announcing the train's arrival over the loudspeakers. The woman shifted her weight from foot to foot in indecision. I moved towards the carriage.

I can watch them for you, I said. Maybe I wanted to help her and maybe I liked that feeling of power. I was the only one who could help her at that moment. The woman was reluctant, she tried to put back the blanket the baby had kicked off and looked around in the carriage for an extra pacifier that was buried among the cloth diapers. The voice came on again, urgent and loud, as if even the artificial amplifier knew that someone need help with a decision.

Finally, she decided, she took a package out of a bag hanging over the carriage handles, looked one last time at me and the children, and ran up the stairs. A few seconds later, a train came noisily into the station.

I leant over the carriage and held my hair back behind my ears so that it wouldn't tickle the child's face and upset him. In the white diapers, the two babies looked like puffed-up pieces of cherry cake arranged on a tablecloth.

At that moment I would have liked to lie around in those white pillows too, just like today, intoxicated by the smell of milk, lulled by the enveloping love of my mother, quiet, unaware and innocent, with underdeveloped senses which would protect me more than they would open up the world to me. I would curl up into a ball like a kitten, bury my face in a diaper and, in almost obligatory infantile inactivity, wait out my entire childhood. I would wake up as an adult, capable of refusing, defending myself and making decisions without any signs. I would prefer to wake up in a different world than the one I had worked my way into in reality. I would like to try living another life. I would find myself transported to my garden hut, in the sparkling morning light, surrounded by little things associated with stories from short periods of happiness. High stalks of hard, long uncut grass would protect me from danger like soldiers. The hedge with its spiny branches sticking out in all directions would protect me. Until I decided of my own will to mow it or cut it, until I was able to defend myself.

I envied children because they didn't have to worry about anything. All they had to do was cry if they wanted something. Somebody always came. Crying loudly is easy though, what's difficult is not crying. What's difficult is swallowing your sadness and fear and loneliness and insecurity while suffocating with a stoneface, only because it's not proper to burden others with it, because there's no good moment, time, or mood for it.

When a baby whimpers, the whole family immediately comes together and everyone wonders whether it's hungry or cold, whether it has pooped or peed, is bored or uncomfortable. Until they begin to think and speak, everyone will say that their crying is normal, natural, even necessary so that they get along with the little ones. With laughter they will say, you keep screaming my little darling, stretch your lungs. Inside though, they wish for the crying to be as brief as possible so that this heart-wrenching wailing doesn't spill out onto the street and the neighbours don't think the parents cannot control their own child. The air thickens and the nerve fibres of these adults begin to vibrate like strings.

I envied their cleanliness, the white nappies, soft blanket embroidered in fine stitches with the monogram of a clothing label. I imagined their mother toiling with a needle and embroidering thread, emotional over the tiny letters. With love those embroidered letters would sit like little guardian angels on the nappies reminding the world what a devoted mother she was, because she'd rather embroider than launder T-shirts, wash her hair or take a nap. Maybe it was the work of the grandmother, the fairytale grandmother who sat by a little window for days, dedicating those rare moments of lucidness, and all the special skills that she had no other use for, to her grandchildren.

I envied them their deep and peaceful sleep and that they could sleep where and when they wanted. After all, everyone is happy when children fall asleep. Then everyone walks around on tiptoe, doors are closed and curtains drawn so as not to wake them. I envied them that everyone would wash their hands when they wanted to hold them and no sweaty adult would climb into their carriage, lie around under their covers and drool yellow saliva on their sheets while they slept.

They were so small, that surely no one put any conditions on loving them. No one said to them, if you're good, we'll love you.

I looked in the bag hanging from the handles of the carriage. It was full of many things: a thermos, powdered milk measured out in transparent plastic bags, plastic measuring cups, extra clothes, disposable nappies, some medicines in little bottles and nose drops too with a soft rubber dispenser. Everything was clean, exemplarily packed in a soft bag, which the woman had forgotten to close. I wondered whether these children were travelling somewhere or whether this was normal preparation for every walk they took, and I was surprised how many things such small children need. I myself, aside from my keys and wallet, carried nothing, not even tissues.

People burdened with packages and suitcases suddenly poured out of the station. I pushed the carriage slightly to the side, deeper into the shade of the newsstand so that no one would bump into it and wake up the children. I looked closely at every traveller, but the woman wasn't among them. I couldn't remember her face exactly, even though I had seen it only a few minutes ago, but I would have recognized her by her torn T-shirt. No one noticed us, neither me nor the big carriage. Two or three people stopped at the newsstand, but when they saw that the grate was down, they left without a word. After a little while the pavement was empty. The stairway and long hallway as well. Not a trace of the woman.

She'd left both of her babies alone. In front of the awful railway station where strange people loitered in the shade of the newsstand, a patch of shade that was mercilessly growing smaller.

The sun was already beating down into the babies' faces and they had begun to frown and get angry, one of them pulled the pacifier out of its mouth with a sudden, uncontrolled movement, the other began to pull strongly at its own. I pushed the carriage away so the sun wouldn't roast them and took the blanket off their naked little legs. Their legs were fat and white with deep folds, as if someone had tied them below the knees with a string. One of them suddenly let out a yell. I tried very hard for a little while to rock them, to walk up and down with the carriage as much as the shade allowed, but the one wouldn't quiet down, and the babies just bumped up and down. I ran up the steps and looked up and down the hallway, but there was no trace of the woman. The voice on the loudspeaker announced the arrival of a train. I returned to the children, who had calmed down in the meantime and were now only whimpering and shaking their little fists. The wind came up, making the leaves rustle on some low bushes. I put my two forefingers into their palms and both closed over them like claws.

The train left. But the woman didn't come back. The babies lay there looking up at the sky. Under the staircase, the wind knocked over an empty beer can flinging it rattling down the pavement, and the aluminium of the can, together with the bubbles in the asphalt and the wind, created a rare melody. I listened. The sound was pleasant and reminded me of the garden because there was often a similar rattling from the other side of the fence. It came from one of the neighbouring gardens, where cans were hung from the trees to scare off crows and jackdaws.

I stood under the stairs and looked into the hall. I realized that no one had come out of the station for a long time. It was odd because before the woman with the carriage came, there had been a constant trickle of people regardless of whether there was a train at the platform or not. Now the station was empty and if there was anyone there, they must have been sitting silently on a bench or leaning against a counter guzzling station beer. It was as if time had stopped in mid-tick. I clearly heard the can hitting the bubbles in the asphalt, heard the clink-clanking, but nothing interrupted that clink-clanking. Not the loudspeaker voice, whistle, clattering wheels, people walking, nothing but a silent pause for the can.

The woman still didn't come back. It seemed to me that she'd been gone for at least an hour, but I had no way of verifying it, I didn't even know what time it was or had been when the train came. I didn't have a phone, it wasn't very common then. Now what? I could stand outside the station for as long as I liked, withstand hunger and thirst, what if the children got hungry, needed a nappy change or started to be bored? If the sun shone on them, they'd get sunstroke. Forgotten, tiny, terrified babies with sunstroke.

I Jarka, who knew very well what it meant to find myself alone with only a few provisions in a plastic bag and a bunch of keys in my pocket, I was the one who would save them. Because if Jarka knows how to take care of herself, of Mama and Irena, she'll know how to take care of these children too. She can take the children somewhere where the racket of the train and the speeding cars won't disturb them, somewhere where they will calm down. She knows how to take care of everything, she'll take care of them too.

If the woman doesn't come back before the beer cans roll up to my feet, I'll take the children away from here. That's how I decided.

Thirteen years later, Dorota, Peter's daughter, had suddenly called me. As a meeting place she chose the Vineyard Railway Station and I didn't understand why. Why didn't she come by car, why wasn't her father picking her up at the Main Station? Why did she think of me?

I waited for her at the station. Nothing had changed in the area. In the city, garages had become a precious commodity, but no one cared about the ones on the edge of town and so their roofs continued to sag, and their half-open gates banged in the wind the same as they had before. The buildings had new facades, three or four new ones were built, one was still under construction. On some parts of the road there was a new carpet of asphalt. Two old walnut trees had been cut down and the young ones had not yet managed to bear fruit.

The ground by the last garages was criss-crossed with cracks. The gaps between the concrete panels were still full of soil from the vineyards. It happened every year. Heavy rains brought dirt down from the vineyards and the wind blew it back up. Behind the garages the path turned into asphalt, freely rising and twisting, lined on one side by grapevines, on the other by a neglected drainage ditch. Water flooded from it in some stretches after a heavier rain, but 5 to 10-metres further down the road it poured back into a shallow ditch. Willows with ears of curly black fungus on them grew along the canal. Above the last row of vines the road divided like a three-pronged fork, and its three arms were so narrow that one car could barely get through. They divided individual gardens from each other. The gardens were long—they were separated from the road by high wire fences and from each other by hedges, wooden planks, raspberry bushes or just a verbal agreement.

Miletic had his at the end of the road and the garden was thoroughly separated from the rest of the world by thick box-wood bushes. They said he was an outstanding gardener—patient, clever and knowledgeable. I believed that he had found a refuge from Comrade Director Irena in the garden, a quiet corner where no one bothered him, ordered him around or breathed down his neck. He renewed the dilapidated hut with blue paint and formed a path with stones. After he emigrated, the garden went to seed.

The grape leaves were rustling, tempting me to continue along the road. I knew that dusty, ripe grapes and edible chestnuts awaited me. And memories inside them like coiled-up worms. Dorota was waiting for me, she had surely got off the train already, because the train had arrived in the meantime. So I turned and ran back, among the garages, the houses, up the slope. I didn't look behind me once. I didn't turn into a pillar of salt.

Two airy kisses on the cheeks, an appropriately light squeeze of the shoulders. Now it's done Parisian-style, elegantly. Slumping children in hoodies touch knuckles and stretch their fingers, everyone in his own way, complicated and effective. So that no strangers will infiltrate these groups of children who can't even see each other's faces for the hoods. When we were younger and we met someone we knew on the street, we didn't know what to do with our hands.

What's up? How are you? What have you been doing all these years? She asked me immediately, as she got off the train and I, despite having prepared some answers ahead of time— what else could someone like Dorota ask?—remained in the gap between reality and expectation. Well, there's so much, I don't know where to begin, and you? I avoided answering. But after a moment it came out—against my will, of course— that it was all crap. And I felt embarrassed, because I didn't take the trouble to lie.

I thought you would look different, she said then, after she had looked me up and down. Hmm, really? Is it better or worse? It can always be worse, I thought to myself. How? It could be worse, no? I said out loud. She patted me on the shoulder again with a gesture that suited her.

It definitely wasn't bad at that time. I was making decent money and a friend of mine in a fashion designer's atelier was making my clothes for me. She used me instead of the plastic figures in the window. She said I had a nice long neck and that it made clothes look good on me. I put away my cargo pants after the first humiliating work interview and decided that I liked to wear dresses. They propped up my extremely damaged self-confidence. Luckily, I hadn't inherited Lucia's love of tiger-skin leggings and gold-plastic appliqué. It could definitely be worse.

And how are you? I asked, when we got into the car. I'm fine too. So now it's behind us. The obligatory phrases that were produced without being taken seriously. In one ear and out the other. And when the phrases have already been said, the air gets heavier. I wondered whether one of us would make up some excuse to leave, or whether we'd end up after midnight in my flat or at some bar in an empathetic hug. I couldn't guess at this point. I couldn't exactly say that I didn't care. She was Peter's daughter, after all. She had appeared truly unexpectedly.

At the intersection in front of the President's Palace, my gearshift slipped and the car jumped. Dorota coughed, she'd swallowed her mint candy. And how is Peter? It just came out of me out of nowhere. Peter? You mean my father? He's here. Where? Here, in the city. He came back. He's been here four years already. You haven't seen each other yet?

A long, very long pause. Something that had been dormant in me for years woke up and hit me over the head. Everything went black, but I said to myself that it was the unpleasant exhaust from the other cars. I closed the window.

I'm going to dinner with him tomorrow. If you want, you can come with me, I'm sure he'd be happy to see you, said Dorota. You should definitely come.

The babies will definitely like it better in the garden than on the urine-covered pavement in front of the railway station, I said to myself pushing the carriage in front of me. It's peaceful there, you get used to the unruly noise of the city after a while and don't notice it anymore. The garden is a living organism, alive at all levels, alive among the tree branches, in the grass, on the ground, under the ground, under the wooden planks of the hut, in the rainwater barrel and even underneath it.

If I can pull the carriage all the way up, I'll have to air out the hut and shoo the flies away, build a fire in the stove and somehow warm milk for the little ones. There was enough wood at the neighbour's, I could scale the fence and borrow a few logs. The neighbour only came to his garden on weekends, during the week he was at work, so there was nothing to be afraid of. The other neighbours also came only rarely and even if they did, I didn't care because they couldn't see me through the hedge anyway. No one would be looking at the children or waking them up with the growling lawnmower.

When the children have eaten, they'll need to have their nappies changed, be entertained until they get tired and then be put to sleep again. While they're sleeping, I'll cut the grass with the small scythe so I can push the carriage on it better and pick the children some blackberries. And in the evening, I'll decide whether to stay in the hut overnight or take them to the housing complex.

That was the plan I thought up for the coming hours. Lucia had left me money for two days and I didn't expect her to come back. She didn't like small children anyway, their screaming bothered her. She said that children, if they came, should be quickly dealt with and sent on their way, given their freedom, she said.

Stones kept getting caught between the double wheels of the carriage and the babies bumped up and down. This constant shaking on the bumpy road tired them out, both fell into a deep sleep, the pacifier fell out of one's half-open mouth and the other sweated so much that a dark ring of wetness appeared on the sheet under its head.

I couldn't push the carriage up the last 50 metres even in a deep forward bend with my arms straight out in front, so I pulled it instead. Backwards for a while with my gaze fixed on the gate in the distance, on the gap in the hedge. A large part of the city was visible from the road. The towers of the Dimitrovka factory, the concrete buildings, the smokestacks of the refinery sticking up like burning matches, the television tower, swimming pool and railway station. When the wind blew up from the city, I recognized the voice of the station loudspeaker and the braking trains. When it blew the other way, the gardens were quiet and the city far away.

I thought about the clattering trains, the trains whose departures Lucia had noted, thanks to which two children had been left at the station. Machines full of people, enormous, dirty and noisy, wheels hypnotically repeating that clackety-clack, clackety-clack. I thought of the sunlight reflecting on the tracks, the smell of cigarette smoke, of the ground marked with sticky rings from overturned cans of soda, the garbage and strange people. This repulsive image helped me make it up the last few metres of difficult terrain.

In front of the gate, I stopped the carriage and sat down on the ground. The children were fast asleep. The dead cat in its shallow hole. I had completely forgotten about it. It didn't interest me anymore.

When I had rested a little, I pushed the carriage into the garden and stopped it in the shade of the hut. From the gate to the hut we left a path of rolled-down grass. I opened the two small windows and door wide, to air it out. I checked the children up close. I leant down right above their faces and listened to see whether they were breathing. Like small mechanical gadgets. Completely different from all of Lucia's friends who puffed and drooled under my bedcovers. Even they had once been fragile and fragrant, but it was hard to believe.

The children slept a suspiciously long time, but what did I know then about babies? Only what I saw on the street or at a friend's house, where they had younger sisters and brothers. It wasn't a lot. I knew how you had to shake up the milk in the bottle, sterilize the pacifiers, change their nappies and burp them. But eventually I wanted to learn everything.

I let the children sleep, at least it gave me time to clean up the hut, make the bed, shake out the pillows and build a fire in the stove. Everything I had planned to do I did truly well and anxiously, as if the babies' well-being depended on how smooth the folds in the blankets were. I went over to them every once in a while to check whether they were breathing regularly, or breathing at all.

It was incredible. I had two little babies in the garden. Real, live ones. I had become their mama. How could something like this have happened? Simple.

I quickly came to like the role of mother. I was excited, nervous and happy, so happy that I had forgotten about the city, the morning's humiliation and about Lucia. I saw everything as though through a funnel which narrowed around the babies, I saw and heard only the babies. I was proud of myself, even if I hadn't done anything yet except push the carriage up the hill to the garden. I felt grown up, responsible, self-sacrificing and good, like a real mother, like a mother from some First-Grade nursery rhyme. I looked at their round faces close up and those faces seemed beautiful to me, clean and flawless. They had become my children—I had saved them. I was responsible for two real children, not for beetles in a matchbox or a hamster in an aquarium, but for two children who one needed to love and sacrifice for. Suddenly I felt grown up.

I wouldn't be bumming around the complex anymore, aimlessly wandering through the grass and construction sites to make the days pass quicker, to kill time.

I knew very well what it was like to be with strange people alone in the flat, in a strange city where you don't know how to get around. With men who just show up out of nowhere and then leave the same way, dressed in leather jackets and dark hoodies, with tattoos on their backs and arms. With women who don't eat anything and think that children don't need to eat either. In a home where you're not allowed to pull back the curtains and open the windows. Nights in such a home, without keys, without Lucia, in a strange bed without a decent sleep or your own things around you, where nothing works, everything just creeks and moans and the walls whisper at night.

I knew how it felt to be cast aside. At Irena's house for two weeks without clean clothes or fresh underwear. And what am I supposed to do when I have to take care of something urgently? Lucia asked.

I was about seven then, and we were living temporarily in the flat of Lucia's friend who worked as a babysitter somewhere in London. When Lucia called, I had to quickly get dressed and into the blue car that was waiting in front of the entrance. You'll go see Grandma Irena in Dimitrovka. I'll come for you in the evening, she would say it quickly and hang up so that I wouldn't lose any time, so that I would quickly put on my shoes and run down the stairs because the blue car was already waiting with the motor running in front of the entrance. In the car was Lucia's girlfriend who was nice and asked me about school and boys. I was happy that she was so interested in me, and asked so many questions, that I answered happily and truthfully. She dropped me off in front of Irena's building and took off quickly. Irena lived in that horrible flat, where the two of us went to live for a while. She was sick, the neighbour brought her lunches from the elementary-school cafeteria because she herself couldn't even make it to the store. God sent you to me, said Irena when I came, and then immediately gave me some stuff to do.

The ice between Irena and Lucia started to melt slightly when Irena began to faint on and off. Then she began to suspect that she'd need someone around all the time very soon. She would call Lucia and try to arouse some empathy and feeling of responsibility in her. And Lucia knew at once how to use the changes in Irena's physical and mental state.

The first day in Dimitrovka I was quite happy, because this stay at Irena's was a disruption in the slowly passing days leading up to the first day of school. I believed that Lucia would truly come for me in the evening. After all, she probably would have told me otherwise, so that I would pack some clothes, pyjamas and a towel—she wouldn't have sent me away unprepared. Only it hadn't occurred to her at all. That used to happen too. There was a problem in the evening when I wanted to brush my teeth and didn't have anything to do it with. Irena generously offered me her hedgehoggy, toothbrush, but I wouldn't even touch it with my hand, let alone put it in my mouth. So that first night I didn't brush my teeth at all and in the morning, I washed the taste of sleep down with a roll. The next night I tried to brush my teeth with my fingers and the next day I filched 2 Euros from Irena and bought the cheapest, totally straight, monochrome brush I could find.

I didn't like the way Irena's towels smelt or her leftover soap or her feather duvets. I didn't like her butter, even though it had the same wrapping as the one in our refrigerator. I hated Irena's wheezing and her constant requests and orders. Bring me water Jarka, close the curtains, please. That raspy 'please'.

Turn the television off already. Cover my legs, not that way, differently. Take the cover off, it's got warm. Are you sleeping? Aren't you sleeping? Scratch me, I can't reach. And don't call me Grandma, I'm no grandma.

I had to sleep in the same room with her on three cushions from the couch, which slid away from each other beneath me like ice flows in a river, but I had no choice because Irena didn't feel sorry for me and had her flat strictly divided. In the bedroom you sleep, in the kitchen you cook and in the living room you do everything else. No changes, no compromises. Breath interrupted by snoring and long pauses. Irena scratching her forearms, dry peeling skin and dandruff flying through the air, flying into my nose, I gasp for air in front of the eternal light of the miniature altar. The eternal light above the head of the plaster Virgin Mary of Lourdes and the cord, which connects that light to the electricity, running along the rug diagonally across the room, under the pull-out couch I sleep on. I the terrified girl. The cord, along which Irena's diseases crawl, accompanied by years of toxic crabbiness and bile.

Turn off that television, it's already eight o' clock, you should go to bed. In the morning you'll go shopping, but you have to go early because by eight everybody's already touched the bread. Stop squirming, it bothers me. All you do is fidget. Where is that mother of yours? She doesn't show up for weeks, she doesn't call. What have I done to deserve this? That father of hers brought her up that way. It was Miletic. Remember that name. And put some cream on my back Jarka, it's itchy.

At first, I waited on Irena hand and foot, running around the flat with tiny steps, urgently and fearfully because I was afraid that if I didn't do what she wanted, Irena would die, die just like that, collapse on the floor, hit her head on the doorframe and then the blood would flow onto the linoleum, under the door and out onto the stairs and I wouldn't be able to do anything except wait for Lucia who was somewhere making money. At the least sign of resistance, Irena would close her eyes, bow her head, clutch her heart and start breathing fast and I would be off fetching, closing, hanging. The groceries, mail, dishes, cover me, uncover me, help me with my socks, little servant, little helper.

After five days, peevish from her eternal dissatisfaction, repulsed by bad food, and my own dirty clothes which I couldn't even change or wash because at Irena's you only did laundry on Saturdays, I decided to escape.

When Irena fell asleep before lunch, in her nightgown with her hairpins and earrings neatly placed on the night table, I went out quietly and took the tram home. Luckily it was only a few stops, but the enormous fear I felt during those ten minutes corroded the determination and thrill of the escape like salty water.

I sat in the tram alone for the first time, and without a ticket. I rarely took the tram, there was nowhere to take it and no reason. In our housing complex, there was a pre-school, school, paediatrician, hairdresser, a Chinese shop with cheap clothes, a grocery shop and a post office. Lucia and I didn't go for walks on the promenade, to the zoo or to the theatre.

It felt like all the passengers were looking at me and knew very well that I didn't have a ticket, that I had escaped and left a sick Irena with all her illnesses, whether real or imagined. Any one of the passengers could be the ticket-checker, the conductor. Even that nasty little boy kicking the seat in front of him could point to me with his index finger and say—she doesn't have a ticket. Jarka doesn't have a ticket. And she left, she definitely ran away. Catch her and take her back to her grandma. As punishment. As punishment she'll rub Irena's back in the morning and lotion on her cracked feet in the afternoon. For three whole weeks, until school starts.

When this terrifying trip was over, I started running and ran for my life from the little boy and the ticket-checker, from the man who was breathing down my neck behind me, from the driver who looked at me in the rearview mirror, his eyes watery and full of evil. I ran away from Irena, whose teeth I could still hear clinking in the glass. When the tram doors opened, I ran from the fine and the feelings of guilt.

At home, I found two of Lucia's girlfriends. One of them was lying sprawled on Lucia's bed. The second was sitting in my room on the floor among piles of burnt-out lightbulbs and looking closely at the sooty shards.

I thought that Lucia had come back and dropped a tray full of glasses, but when the woman raised her head, two unfamiliar eyes looked at me.

They were two ghosts, trapped in their own private universe. They looked unhealthy and unpleasant and I was afraid of them. Those two and other similar friends came over drunk and tired when they needed somewhere to sleep, or just to rest and talk. They rested in my bed, in the kitchen in a chair, in the bathtub, in the bathroom in the space between the washing machine and the wall, on the steps in front of the door, on the toilet, by Lucia's bed, in Lucia's bed, in Lucia's arms. They came to us to recover, Lucia received them with empathy and understanding like a nun, she gave them food, lent them her things, my things. They came to recover and Lucia took care of them better than she ever took care of me. She fed them and lent them her things, my things. She took care of them better than she did me and I couldn't understand it. Why did I always have to cook for myself, do laundry and then go to Dorota's, why did I have to wait on the stairs while the doors were always open to these guys? I knew that even they would sooner or later get up, dust themselves off, shake it off, wash their face. Perhaps they would clean up a bit, maybe leave some chocolate on the table or some small thing, or they would filch something. I might see them again, or they might never return.

Unlike me, those two brought over everything they needed—clothes, make-up, magazines, cigarettes, music, and food and in two days they managed to fill the flat with their own lives from floor to ceiling.

My expectations of relief at getting home to familiar surroundings and my own bed were replaced by disappointment and fear. I decided on the lesser of two evils and, without a word I packed everything in a bag, drank a glass of water and went out into the hallway. I sat down on the shoe cupboard and for a while, a very short while, I cried. I felt like sleeping, like going into the cupboard among the shoes, taking myself apart like a Lego figure and resting. In the end, I returned to Irena's even before she had woken up.

Lucia came back in two weeks, two days before the start of the school year, and brought me a new school bag, a double-decker pencil case full of pastels and pens, sweet-smelling erasers and stickers, rulers, notebooks, a tracksuit, slippers, all of it in one big box and all of it new and fragrant. I had to try everything out right away and walk around in my new slippers with the school bag on my back in Irena's kitchen, do a handstand in my tracksuit, draw with the ruler, erase Irena's filled-out crossword puzzle and lots of other stupid things.

The two darling, sweet-smelling babies were still lying in the carriage. It wasn't a dream. I didn't make it up. They were there, squirming and opening their fists in their sleep. When they woke up, they'd be hungry. My girlfriend, who had a little sister, said that little children are constantly hungry. If they're not sleeping then they're always eating, and when you don't give them something to eat, they scream. I had to prepare myself for this, had to look in the bags and get everything they needed ready to make the powered milk for them. I found two bottles and four rubber nipple tips that looked totally identical and I didn't know why there were so many of them. I found a plastic measuring cup and a packet of milk, but I didn't find the instructions for how to make it. This hadn't occurred to me.

One of them woke up. The one on the left, the one in blue. Must be a boy. I didn't know for sure because the babies were identical down to the last detail and neither one of them had pierced ears. But there was no time to find out what sex they were and at that moment it wasn't important either. I was excited that I would finally be able to pick it up and talk to it. At that moment, I realized that I had no idea what its name was. It was a dumb surprise and I was suddenly filled with disappointment, because I had ruined something right from the beginning. After all, I should have immediately asked the woman what they were called, after all it's the first question that comes to mind. What's your name? And you? And her?

As long as the children were lying in the carriage, they were like one—one little body, one voice, two sprouts of one plant, siblings. Like with my neighbours from the housing complex, Pete and Mat, no one could tell them apart and they often switched names just to confuse people even more. Not until they woke up was it necessary to divide them from each other and find their names, I couldn't just keep calling them 'my little ones'.

I looked at everything in the bag and the carriage: the nappies, the footsie-pyjamas, socks, little shirts, bags and medicines and finally I did notice that there were Band-Aids stuck on the bottom of the bottles with the names of the children. Jacob and Adele. Such nice names.

I took Jacob by the armpits and carefully lifted him up. I moved very carefully—I was afraid of hurting him if I squeezed his shoulders too hard. First his head fell back quickly, it was frightening because I wasn't used to such movements. It seemed to me that moving like that would definitely damage or break something in his neck. His weight also surprised me, throwing me backwards and off balance. I regained my balance and pressed him against my body. He whimpered, tossing his head around and waving his fists until he accidentally caught a part of my T-shirt and held onto it tightly. So I walked around the garden with him like that, leaning back to keep my balance, and jiggled him up and down. At first, I did it stiffly, and then after a few steps I was softer about it and more relaxed. Afraid that he would make more unpleasant movements, I pressed my cheek to his head and somehow intuitively held the crown of his head with the tips of my fingers. The boy had an oval-shaped bald spot there from lying in the crib and around it were wispy tufts of light-coloured hair. I felt that he wasn't at ease, he was stiff too, hanging from his clutching fingers off my T-shirt like a cat hanging on a curtain in some comic film.

You don't have to be afraid of me little Jacob, I kept saying to him quietly, I'm going to take care of you now, I whispered into his hair. I tried to speak as calmly and naturally as possible, because I knew very well that false calm brings nothing good. The last thing I wanted was to scare the child or lie to him. I murmured to the children the way one normally does. My own voice sounded strange to me, it stuttered. I wasn't used to talking that way, because the time when I used to put dolls and teddy bears to sleep was long behind me. The scent of his body helped me, filled me up, calmed me. With each step, I forgot about everything around me and felt only his smell and his weight. If he weren't so heavy, I would carry him around the garden until all the grass was tramped down flat.

Walking around the garden with my nose pressed into his head, I felt peace and tranquillity. Some kind of odd satisfaction similar to what I had felt in brief moments with Peter, when the three of us sat on the carpet in Dorota's room and played picture-matching memory games together. There was something there at their house that was missing at ours. Everywhere Lucia and I went it was missing, but at Peter and Dorota's house it was there. In the rooms, between the two of them, when they talked to each other, even when they argued. Some invisible fibre, threads that connected the three members of the household and the objects they touched. They were everywhere and it was nice to sink into them. It was good that they let me.

Once I rode with Peter in the car, he took us to the skating rink. It was around the corner, but Peter said that he would drive us, as many children from the building as could fit in the car. I sat in front, because I was the oldest, with my hand on the stick shift—because Peter let me do it, sit in front with my hand on the stick shift—and all the other children were squeezed into the backseat being silly. And I didn't hear them, didn't join in their games, I was waiting to shift gears. When the car took a turn, he put his big hand on mine, then he lightly pressed it, pulled the stick shift and then placed his hand back on the steering wheel. On the open road, he gave me instructions on what to do so that I could change gears properly. He trusted me. And I sat as if in a dream, revelling in the quiet intimacy of our joint driving. Closeness.

I was most often terrified by the thought that Lucia would disappear, that something would happen to her and that she would have done it to herself. I was afraid that she'd leave me alone. I was afraid of the emptiness and the men waiting behind the garage doors. I was afraid that they would come one day and Lucia wouldn't be home. They would lie down next to me in the bed but there wouldn't be anyone home to knock on my bedroom door and send them away, remind them that it's time to take their pills and then get out. And they would finish what Lucia's presence had thus far prevented them from doing, whether intentionally or not. All at once or one after the other.

I was afraid that some day I might find Lucia dead. I would find her. Just like I found Irena. She had died while getting dressed for bed after her bath, with her nightgown hiked up high and turned inside-out, covering her entire face. The bathtub was full of dirty, cold water, the body twisted in the cramped bathroom, legs propped against the door. I had had to wash, dress and scratch that body so many times, the body of an old woman who no one had ever said anything nice about, who people preferred not to talk about at all. Nobody liked her, nobody was excited to come see her, it was always just calculation or obligation to an old woman, to a former director of an elementary school, a mother, a grandmother, neighbour, acquaintance.

Lucia and I took care of her for more than a year, but it was mostly me, just so that we could have somewhere to live. No other reason existed, only that dank flat. Irena was rigid and uncompromising, she liked to talk about morality and custom, she preferred to have her silverware placed on a table-cloth even when eating the most ordinary food. She was tough, so tough and rigid that she let her young and ignorant daughter move from rental to rental, and then when she herself needed her daughter's help, she sent her some money and freed up a room in her flat. And I'm still afraid to open the bathroom door because it might hit someone's hard knee, a body without a face.

There was no fear visible on the baby boy's face. He looked at my face with eyes wide open and carefully watched every movement. I'm not your mama, I repeated to myself. I'm not your real mama, but that's not important now. But you're not afraid of me, are you? So far, I'm just one of those aunties who takes care of you until your real mama comes. She needs to be alone, get on a train and go earn some money. It won't be long before you both forget her. You see, you're not even crying, you're not afraid of me. You just need someone to rock you. I'm not grown up yet, but I know how to take care of myself. I know what's bad for children, I myself am still a child. I'll be acting according to that. I won't be like my mama, I won't pretend that I'm something else, I won't be ashamed of you. I'll give you everything I know how to give.

I took Jacob into the hut. Adele was still fast asleep, breath flowing through her slightly open mouth. I put Jacob down on the bed and surrounded him with pillows so he wouldn't roll onto the tile floor. I stoked the fire in the wood stove. It only took me a moment. I used up all the wood. I filled a pot with water outside and boiled it. While it was cooling, I sat by the boy and watched him trying to roll over onto his stomach. I helped him. I brought him his toys and showed them to him one by one. He smiled, his head bobbing on his neck like a poppy flower. I put a small plastic mouse in his hand and went to check on Adele. I brought her, still sleeping, inside and put her on the edge of the bed so that her brother wouldn't hit her unintentionally. I wanted to have both children by me and wanted them to be happy. I remembered Pete and Mat and how they always clung to each other. When the water cooled, I poured it into the bottles and poured the milk powder into it, estimating the amount until the water turned white. I put one bottle into the rest of the warm water in the pot, I sprayed two or three drops from the other onto my forearm as I had seen other mothers do. The milk was warm, but the truth was that I had no idea whether it was too warm or just right. This made me a bit nervous because I had been sure about that one thing until then and was looking forward to the time when I would, like a veteran mother, roll up my sleeves and test the milk on my wrist.

Jacob drank the milk down in one sitting without crying. I picked him up and carried him upright around the hut until he burped and until Adele woke up crying. She got milk too. She obediently drank it, but when it was finished, she started screaming. Heart-wrenching and surprisingly loud screaming that shot through my head like a nail pounded in with a giant hammer. I had been expecting the babies to cry sooner or later, but the reality was much, much worse and the intensity of the screaming coming out of these mouths as small as keyholes paralysed me. The pacifier, walking around the hut, rocking, singing, toys—nothing worked. She screamed and when I put her on the bed, she kicked her legs, stretched them out and moved like a stiff arrow.

After a bit the boy started too. Suddenly the hut seemed small and overfilled, the air stuffy. I closed the windows and door so that the screaming couldn't be heard outside, put both children next to each other on the bed and lay down with them. I clenched my teeth and pulled them to me. Their screaming thrashed my ears, but I held on, because something told me that this was the way to quiet children down. Their bodies shuddered, their tongues shaking in their mouths. Now their voices were the same, only Adele sobbed more when she cried. For ten minutes we drowned in the common current of their screaming. I closed my eyes and tried to feel only the warmth of their shuddering bodies and not their wailing. I steeled myself and after a while, the crying stopped being so loud, as if it weren't coming from these children lying next to me but from somewhere farther away, from under a glass bell. I opened my eyes and looked at the alarm clock. It was a little before twelve, the second hand was just passing the three. If the children were still shrieking like sirens when both hands joined at the twelve, I would have to do something.

Just then, as if on command, Jacob stopped screaming, suddenly interested in the lace of my hoody and two or three minutes later Adele started coughing and choking on the milk that was coming back up into her mouth. I jumped up from the bed, picked her up high and shook her, it was the only thing that occurred to me quickly. A white stream of undigested milk shot out of her mouth and hit the ground with a splat like a wet rag. Adele tried to catch her breath, but the milk that she hadn't spit up yet was gurgling in her throat, flowing out of her nose and choking her. I wanted to tip her forward so that it would flow out by itself, because I remembered how Lucia had once held my head over the sink when my nose was bleeding. Adele was heavy and my arms, tired from so much carrying, refused to serve me. I couldn't hold her in the air and so I just shook her until all the milk flowed out onto my face, my sleeves and the ground. The girl then went quiet, terrified and tired, wet with sweat, milk and saliva. I put her on the bed and put a pillow under her head. I wiped her and myself off with a clean nappy. Her face was read and blotchy, her eyes swollen. I lay down with her, head-to-head, so that I could hear whether she was breathing regularly, whether she was choking. She was still shuddering, but with each breath she shook less. I began to cry, my tension relaxed.

We lay close for a long time, like kittens, two small children and I. Jacob rolled over onto his belly, murmured to himself, nodded his head and hit my slightly open palm with a plastic toy. Adele fell asleep again. As she slept, her face regained its original healthy pink colour, cooled down and looked better. It was nice to observe her, her rhythmically moving pacifier and tiny earlobes. It was nice to just lie there playing with the little boy's fingers and making him laugh with a toy. I calmed down. I stopped shaking and closed my eyes. I thought of Peter, of how he was always in control. Of his tranquillity, which overflowed like a river onto its surroundings and eroded the nervousness of everyone around him. I thought about Dorota, dressed up as a baby for the pre-school carnival, wrapped in a big stuffed nappy, with a pacifier made of sugar in her mouth.

I thought about Lucia. About the evening when she had drunk a bit and felt like talking. Irena was laid out in the funeral parlour white and terrifying, but safely stiff. It was pitch black outside, only the lights from the windows of the house opposite us were lit like lamps. The light was on in Maya's room, and in the twins' room too. A lace tablecloth hanging on the neighbour's clothesline was slapping against the window.

Lucia was trying to be gay and relaxed. She poured me a glass of wine and I drank it all. It's just like fruit drink, she said. You can drink it, it'll help you fall asleep. She was talking about herself, but the whole time I had the feeling she was talking about someone far away, just reproducing a story told a hundred times by gossiping women.

It had to go fast . . . Lucia said, and sipped her wine . . . Because there were four other women squeezing their legs together waiting for the maternity ward, it was a population explosion . . . Lots of babies . . . just like you . . . we waited for the table like they waited in line for oranges, we slept on cots. It was demeaning, so demeaning . . . I've never been through anything worse. They yelled at me, Jesus, she must be stupid, she doesn't know how to push, she's stupid and young, someone jump on her again and help her out, let the kid come out! After two days, they sent me home because they needed the bed. I couldn't walk and no one came to get me. Who would have come for me? An ambulance driver took me . . . I wanted to invite him in at least for coffee, he was handsome and smelt good, finally after all that suffering someone who would talk to me normally . . . but Irena threw him out, sent him away saying that there would be no cabaret in the flat, it was enough that the two of us had come back from the hospital. Can you imagine? . . . I was so terribly clueless . . . It wasn't until the fifth month that I figured out I was pregnant and then it was already too late for an abortion . . . they only do it until the fourth month . . . I was sixteen. The connections that Irena thought were so valuable didn't help. Her doctor friends . . . she had friends everywhere . . . but the midwife-sorceresses too, the ones who performed abortions on the kitchen table with sterilized scissors, they refused to clean me out . . . She left me at home, merciful . . . Until I had carried to term and healed and found some hole to live in. She hid me, so that no one knew, I couldn't go out. When it was time to go for a check-up, she threw her big coat over my shoulder so my belly wouldn't be visible, got into a taxi with me and watched me like the Gestapo, so that I couldn't dawdle anywhere, so that I wasn't seen anywhere unnecessarily. For three months I sat in my room. At school, she arranged everything, one phone call was enough. Two weeks after the birth, we were already living at a girlfriend's house, you slept in the pram, or next to me on the floor in an army sleeping bag. In a month, I was working in the kitchen. When I wasn't greasing pans, I was nursing you. I had you in a carriage, parked in the hall by the bathrooms. Then I lost my milk and from then on my girlfriend took care of you. At least I didn't feel like a milk cow. What are you looking at . . . what was I supposed to do . . . the father? You think I knew who it was? There were six or seven of them, guys studying at the mechanical-engineering vocational school . . . they had me in the equipment closet in the school gym, where they kept the mats and balls . . . we let ourselves be locked in there after a co-ed civil-defence exercise . . . we unscrewed the light bulb . . . one after the other . . . in the dark . . . I don't remember much . . . only the echoes . . . but it wasn't so bad . . . I had definitely been through worse . . . it was just for fun. I didn't want to point the finger at anyone. Can you imagine? They would line them up in front of me like convicts ready for the firing squad and one of them would take the heat . . . and I would have to marry him to boot. For sure! Married to some metalworker! How was I supposed to know which one it was? In the end, I didn't even remember anything, I had drunk half a bottle of muscatel beforehand. We stole it from some army guy who was handing out gas masks. I only remember those sounds . . . how you could hear everything in there . . . the leather mats squeaked . . . I'll never forget that. How those leather mats squeaked in the dark.

Lucia drank straight from the bottle and put her hair up in a bun. Then she sat silently, with her hands in her lap. A wet string hit the window regularly. Drip, drip, drip, buzz, buzz.

I'll tell you what your grandma did. When I was in my eighth month, she sent me to some Vietnamese woman from the embassy to iron shirts. I must have ironed a hundred shirts in one day, with that big belly and swollen feet I stood at the ironing board from eight in the morning until six at night ironing some stranger's rags. So that I could earn money for new things and for rent. I lasted for three weeks, then they took me away.

Ever since then, you don't iron, I said.

Ever since then, I don't iron, she said.

Drip, drip, drip. She poured water into my still-unfinished glass of wine. I was sleepy. I was tired. And probably drunk. Lucia was tired. As if after a big fight. After a big fight with Irena, which we, like it or not, had won together. There were few occasions where we shared things.

When I returned with you from the maternity ward, there was a new wall unit in my children's bedroom, varnished birch veneer . . . full of knick-knacks, glasses and rainbow fish, as if they'd been there for years . . . you know how it looks when something's been somewhere forever . . . two chairs, a small table, on the table a crocheted cloth, starched, white . . . on the cloth a bowl of walnuts. My toys, books, plastic cups, posters, old school notebooks, nothing was left, she had thrown everything away . . . she'd had the walls painted, they were still damp, when we came . . . my bed . . . my clothes . . . your footsie pyjamas and nappies . . . imagine, Jarka . . . she sewed a thick curtain . . . took great care that it went with the carpet, lovely, the length and width precise . . . she hung it in the kitchen and behind that curtain she hid us. My bed and clothes were in three bags. She hid us behind a curtain like a vacuum cleaner. Like some garbage. So that we would get out as soon as possible. So that I would realize that I didn't have a bedroom anymore, that I was just an appendage.

The only daughter of an elementary-school director had let some boys from the vocational school knock her up. Her only daughter didn't have a diploma. She didn't get married. Everyone got married then. It didn't matter to whom, but you got married. Otherwise you were easy, or something like that . . . a slut . . . And I didn't get married. I was that stupid one and I stayed stupid . . . and you will also be stupid because you have no intelligent relatives to take after, Jarka. I'm sorry . . . whatever . . . I don't care. Go to sleep already, at least you can be pretty for the funeral tomorrow.

Lucia put her hands on the table, head on her arms. She closed her eyes.

Lucia, come and get into bed, I said.

Leave me be, she whispered so quietly that I could barely understand her.

I got into *her* bed and waited. I dozed with the children for a little while but was awoken by a blow from the plastic toy that flew out of Jacob's hand by mistake. While I was sleeping, he had managed to turn over onto his back.

The boy was in constant motion. He didn't put his arms and legs down on the bed for a second, he turned his head back and forth as if it were held on by a joint full of ball bearings, and if I managed to hold his attention with a toy for a longer time, he screwed up his face, gathered himself up and kicked and kicked. His movements were undirected, more or less random, he only managed to put his hand on the toy I offered him once in a while. Any piece of paper, clothing label or embroidery on a pillow was enough to keep him happy. I felt as if I could play with him like that my whole damn life, that it's really easy to take care of one or two, of all the children in the world.

I hung a hanger with some string on it over the bed and from it I hung some unripe apples, pieces of coloured paper, feathers and a spoon. That took care of Jacob's entertainment for another half hour. I had to pee. I ran out of the hut and peed in the grass.

I gathered some blackberries. They were sweet and soft and made purple stains on my hands. Blackberries had a lot of vitamins, I said to myself, they definitely can't hurt the children, they can't just gulp milk all the time. There's not that much of it anyway, I have to be thrifty with it. I stuffed so many blackberries into my mouth at once that I couldn't move my tongue at all. I laughed and the berries exploded into the tall grass.

With the blackberries in my mouth, I was filled with a feeling of indescribable happiness and I laughed, laughed out loud with my head thrown back and one big blackberry imprisoned under my tongue. I fell into the grass. The sun was shining directly into my face, I closed my eyes. I felt like a swimmer, waves of grass carried me along and I could only see for short moments a blue smoking steamboat in-between the waves, the boat from my dreams. In the boat lay two little castaways, I had never been to the sea, but this is how I imagined that drifting feeling of comfort by the sea.

I stuffed the remaining blackberries into my mouth, I wiped my hands on the grass. Under my right hand I felt a hard bump. It took me a long time until I remembered what this flaw in the regularly woven carpet of grass was, what that mound hid. The sad episode with the dead cat seemed so far away and foggy that it was hard to believe it had happened only yesterday. The cat's body in its little grave definitely still looked like a cat. Perhaps it was more smashed and dusty, but it was still a cat.

Annoyed, I got up and thoroughly washed my hands in the rainwater barrel, because I felt like I was contaminated with something unhealthy. On the way back to the hut, I picked a few more blackberries.

I was hungry. I remembered the last roll that was still wrapped in the plastic bag. On the shelf I found a jar of home-made apricot jam. I sat down on the bed frame by Jacob, the objects turning above him on the strings. Jacob stretched his arms up to them, rolled his eyes, but only rarely managed to coordinate his hands and eyes such that he caught the swing-ing spoon. I dipped the roll into the jam. I also put one finger into the jam and then into Jacob's mouth. His toothless gums were hard, the pressure of the boy's jaw was surprisingly strong. I stuck my finger into my mouth and felt my own gums.

Everything about the babies was interesting. I had never had the opportunity to be so close to other people, to touch them without them commenting on it. The children lay next to me, they were defenceless, they didn't protest. I wasn't a problem. I wasn't stupid. They didn't judge my actions, didn't tell me—they didn't even show me with their eyes—that I was dumb, annoying or impolite and I squeezed their earlobes, smelt their hair—again and again—picked them up, weighed them in my hands, squeezed them. With them I felt pleasantly warm.

I scraped the last of the jam from the jar and gave it to Jacob to lick again. He frowned, stuck out his pointy tongue and tried to reach the jar. I squashed a big blackberry between my fingers and gave him a taste of that too. He spit it out, but in my opinion, it was sweet, so I pushed it into his mouth again.

Blackberries are full of vitamins. Vitamins are necessary for healthy development, I said to him.

It was one-thirty. An hour and a half had passed since the last feeding. More than twenty-four hours since my last real meal. For dinner I'd had yogurt, for breakfast, two plain rolls. For lunch, one roll with jam and blackberries. My stomach began to hurt.

I realized that I would have to find some food somewhere, but by the time I had figured out a plan, Adele had woken up very noisily. Suddenly, without warning and for no apparent reason, she let out a heart-wrenching yell. Jacob was frightened by it as well, but it sufficed to take him over to the carriage and rock him a bit and he then found a string and a piece of paper to quietly focus on.

With Adele it was more difficult. She twisted and turned sharply and all the strength that had managed to gather in her during the few months of her life she now used to try to slip out of my embrace, to push me away and hit me. I couldn't leave her on the bed because she could fall, and I couldn't even manage to hold her. I managed to the put the blanket on the floor and fix it with my foot and then I left the screaming child on it. Adele yelled until she choked. I ran around her showing her toys, stroking her, picking her up and putting her down again. When she got stuck and cramped up and suddenly stopped crying and breathing, I shook her, as much as I could, so that she would come around and catch her breath.

When that didn't help anymore, I ran outside, as if I were expecting that somewhere in the grass, or on a tree, I would find a miraculous toy which would calm the child, I exhaled deeply in front of the hut. My whole body was shaking. Then it occurred to me that she must be hungry again and so I ran inside again, poured the almost cold water into an unwashed bottle and very quickly mixed in the milk powder. Adele was turning from side to side and by the time I managed to get the nipple into her mouth, her whole face was wet, her eyes full of milk, milk on her clothes, down her neck. She started to choke again, but I said to myself that if I held the bottle in her mouth and didn't take notice of her coughing, she would understand that the milk was flowing down her throat and start drinking normally.

Adele had no choice but to swallow the whitened water. When she had drunk half the bottle, she pushed the nipple out with her tongue and gave a strange gurgling cough. Milk began to flow from her nostrils. She began to choke again, but she was already so tired, that she let me pick her up and carry her facedown, turned to the floor. The floor was covered with milk, I had kicked the bunched-up blanket into the corner so that I wouldn't trip on it. There were toys scattered every-where, the now unlit wood stove was covered with white powder and the hut was full of smoke.

Adele calmed down. She was wet and needed to be changed. I put her on her belly in case the milk started to come up again, I surrounded her with toys. I ran outside to check on Jacob. Jacob had also turned onto his belly in the carriage and I could only hope that he wouldn't fall out.

I thought it would definitely be better if I had them both in my sight so that I wouldn't have to run back and forth all the time. I had to admit that it was dawning on me that two babies were really a bit much for me, but I still thought it was just beginner's nerves that would pass as soon as they were full, dry and changed. Then there would be time for playing and cuddling. The reality was, however, completely different. As soon as I had changed Adele successfully and without any major problems, Jacob, who was supposed to be changed two hours before, wet his nappy completely. While I was changing Jacob's nappy and clothes, Adele started crying again and the only thing that helped was to carry her around and bounce her up and down. While an unhappy Jacob was whimpering in the carriage, I walked around the garden with Adele. I waded through the tall grass and told myself that when I had a moment, I would cut the grass in at least part of the garden so that I wouldn't have to work so hard to walk around and at least this baby-lulling process would be enjoyable for me.

My plan was to put the children down to sleep on the bed in the afternoon, cut the grass and go find some food, wash everything and rest. I was starting to be tired and sleepy. My stomach hurt. I had at least eaten some blackberries, but only to fill my empty belly. When I couldn't carry Adele around anymore, I put her in the carriage and pulled both babies around the garden, which was pretty difficult thanks to the tall grass and stones. The stalks of grass got tangled in the wheels and the carriage was heavy and clumsy.

The wild bumping of the carriage finally put the babies to sleep. I parked them in the shade of the hut. It was three-thirty. It had grown cooler and the sky had clouded over. My stomach was already hurting me so much that I couldn't think of anything else. And in the hut, other than a bottle of ketchup, I hadn't found anything to eat. The apples weren't ripe yet, the gooseberries had fallen off the bush before they were ripe and my stomach turned at the thought of more blackberries. The only thing I could think of was to look in the neighbour's hut. I had to decide quickly because the children could wake up again. I had already given up hope of them sleeping the way I had imagined and needed, like twins—at the same time, like twins—long and peacefully.

I climbed over the fence, broke the window with a stone, crawled in through the window and looked around the hut. In the cupboard I found twenty-four cans of fish and about fifty cans of something I didn't recognize. Judging from the design of the goods, they came from the ancient past, judging from the writing on the cans, from a foreign country. I left a hunk of sour-smelling bacon covered in a white coating hanging behind the door and took a package of pasta with me. I also threw a few armfuls of wood, a big empty cardboard box and a clean basin over the fence. I put the wood in the box and left the basin outside.

I made pasta with ketchup to the sound of a whimpering, newly awoken Adele. I had to carry her around the hut again so Jacob wouldn't wake up too. I got nervous. Adele was meowing like a hungry cat, the fire in the stove had gone out again and the hut was filling with acrid smoke. I just couldn't get the pasta into my mouth.

I felt somehow cooped up in the garden as well. I needed to run a bit, break free from the pressure of my emotions, cool down my nerve-endings, which, after two months of holidays, had suddenly begun to work at full speed and solve a lot of problems. I didn't dare leave the children alone, but when Adele started to complain at full volume again for no apparent reason, I couldn't stand it and, like a crazy person, I ran out onto the road and down the hill to the railway station. After about 100 metres, my head was clear enough for me to get hold of myself and shoot back up.

I remembered the day I had found Irena in the bathroom. As if turned to stone, I stared from the bathroom doorway at her thin, wrinkled legs. I stuck a slipper under the door, so that it wouldn't fly open under the pressure of those bent legs and show me the whole body. Then something clicked in my head, as if two magnets had found the proper position, and I began to slowly and soberly think about the next steps.

Irena was dead and naked. It wasn't a pretty sight. The worst thing was that I couldn't see her face. It was as if it wasn't even my Grandma Irena. It was just a body without a head, leaning against the washing machine.

I covered her with a white sheet, for which the emergency medical people, whom I then called, praised me. First, I reached the fire station, which, given my age and situation, could not be considered a mistake. I didn't touch anything, for which the police, who had been called by the firemen, praised me. I turned off the electric heater, I still don't know why. I told the police that the neighbour was taking care of me and that I'd wait at her house until my mother came. No one confirmed this. They didn't send me for any psychological support. While they were in the flat, I waited on the landing above our floor and pretended to be talking with the neighbour. Then I returned home, took a 100-note from under Irena's mattress and went to buy some cola and French fries. I waited for Lucia on the stairs, I didn't want to stay in the flat for anything.

The run down the hill did me good. My anxiety disappeared, and the crying didn't sound so horrible anymore. With a clear head, I made the meowing Adele some milk and took all the dirty dishes outside. I left them in the basin by the water tap, hoping that I would manage to wash them before I found myself short of dishes. On the way back in, I checked on the sleeping Jacob.

It was like a ride on a big merry-go-round. You continually think about the same things, in the same order and in intervals that are too short, so that during the ride you quickly become overwhelmed and tired. All the joy is lost in the speed. I couldn't hope for anything more than a look at the sleeping Jacob, at his slightly open mouth and quickly rising chest, because I had to give Adele her bottle. When she had finished drinking, I carried her in an upright position around the whole garden, so that the milk would run down into her stomach and not come up from where it was supposed to be. After two episodes of her choking, I understood that Adele's stomach was like a pot without a cover, which couldn't hold the liquid inside it. The only thing that helped was carrying her in my arms.

While I was carrying Adele around, Jacob had to be by himself. Thanks to his very functional stomach, he was agile and strong and could turn onto his stomach and back. I had to make sure he didn't roll off the bed and upset the carriage. I had to have eyes in back of my head and do several things at once.

At six o'clock I made the last of the milk. This time it was Jacob's turn, so he got the bottle. The coloured water didn't satisfy him very much, he started to be unhappy and irritated from hunger and even the pacifier didn't help. And that was very troubling, because until then he'd been my little sunshine who had calmed me down with his cuddliness and warmth. I had to find some milk.

I left the children in the hut. I wound a string around Jacob's waist and tied it to one end of the bed so he wouldn't fall, Adele I barricaded at the other end among the blankets and toys. I put out the glowing embers in the stove and closed the windows. I threw a piece of corrugated metal over the carriage so it wouldn't be visible. I closed the gate and locked it. I headed deeper into the garden colony. I stopped at each fence and decided how likely it was for the owners to keep long-life milk in their garden huts. Surprising as it was for the end of August, and during the harvest season, the gardens were almost empty. In the distance, I could only see two smoking fires. Someone was getting rid of the first fallen leaves or some homeless people were making goulash. I didn't know what would be better to do—try to break a window on a locked hut that I knew was often visited by elderly pensioners or rob an open hut whose owners were picking grapes.

First, I tried a hut belonging to an old woman who was on her knees pulling weeds in- between her rows of vegetables. I didn't stand there thinking for long but jumped, crouching down behind some flowering hibiscus bushes, all the way to the hut with its door wide open, inviting me to come look inside. I looked through the cupboards in the improvised kitchen, boxes of onions, plastic bags, buckets. No milk anywhere, not even anything to eat.

Old people live on air and memories, like Irena, I thought in disappointment and took a 100-note from a wallet that was lying on the table just in case. I only hesitated for a moment. With Indian hops I got back behind the woman's back to the road and continued on. I hurried, but even so, it seemed to take an eternity and other than the money, which the children couldn't eat, I didn't have anything.

At the end of the garden plots, I discovered a fixed-up, freshly painted hut with no bars on the windows. I broke a small window, crawled inside and found spices, flour, some pickled vegetables, a lighter and three beers. I took only the lighter and the flour. I kicked the broken glass off the veranda into some wilting lobelia.

I continued on along the terraces among the vines until I got to a detached overgrown garden which jutted like a peninsula into the vineyard. A small stream of smoke was coming from the middle of the peninsula. I walked along the fence until I found a hole. On the other side of the fence, among the hazelnut trees and overgrown grapevines, some kind of plants and corn were growing, plants that were unusual for the area. You could crawl into the middle of the garden through the hard stalks of corn. I left the flour in its paper wrapping in the grass so I could have my arms free to move better. In the middle of the overgrown island stood a house made of corrugated metal and boards, next to it was some kind of drying space where bunches of grass were hanging, in front of the drying room was an old writing desk with the drawers ripped out and at the table sat two men of about twenty, who were sorting the dried bunches of plants, or cutting them or grinding them or whatever they were doing. They were smoking. They didn't speak to each other, just took the crumbling stalks in their hands and pulled the leaves off them, intent as two monks. I watched them for a while, but their activity was even less interesting than the old woman's weeding. They weren't even cute. All pimples and grimy dark clothing. Just like Lucia's friends. I found about a half-litre of long-life milk in an open box and some other half-eaten groceries in a crate that was lying in the grass between the hut and the drying room. A crate that used to hold chocolate-wafer cookies Crawling to the drying room and taking the milk was probably about as difficult as going to the supermarket and leaving without paying. I had experience and was really hungry, and that was enough. I took two peanut-butter wafers and stuffed them in my shirt.

I ran back down the road. As I was more or less successfully finishing my mission, the August sky grew dark and clouded over with an unbroken layer of steel-grey clouds. Dusk began to fall over the grapevines, and it grew cooler. It put me in a bad mood, because the coming evening didn't bode well for me. I still hadn't decided whether to stay with the children in the garden hut or take them to the housing complex. Sometimes the power went out here in the garden colony, and after a big storm the garden was flooded. It didn't look like a storm, though, more like light, persistent rain.

I slowed down—I had a pain in my side. Through the gap in the bushes, I looked down at the city, at the train tracks that curled around the vineyards like a snake, and thought about Lucia. What she might be doing, how she was feeling. But she was as far away as some misty, long ago dream. An old, preserved battleship anchored deep in the memory, waiting for sailing orders.

While I was away, it had grown quite dark in the hut and I had to turn on the light so I could find the children. A yelling Jacob was balanced on the edge of the bed, his head lolling in the air like a red radish balanced on the edge of a table. The string had come off and was tangled somewhere around his knees. I pulled Adele out from under the pillows and toys. She was sweaty, but otherwise looked normal. I hugged and kissed both of them for a long time and carried them in my arms one after the other and whispered into their cold ears the story of my food mission. I changed their nappies. I was excited to be with them.

The carrying, lifting and changing went extremely well this time, and the children didn't seem as heavy or fragile to me as they had in the beginning. For a half an hour we played on the bed, during this time I ate both peanut wafers and drank from the box of milk. It was already dark outside. I had hung a blanket over the window so that it wouldn't be visible that the light was on inside the hut. When I saw that the children were calm, I went outside for a while and sat on the grass.

The grass was damp from a light, cold rain and it was cool outside. Summer was already definitely ending; summer always ended on the first of September. The sky was lit by the lights of the city, neither black nor blue, just dirty and somehow empty. I thought then that it was normal to see only twenty or thirty stars in the sky. And that everyone in the world, on both hemispheres saw the same cloudy coffee, that coffee that is the normal night sky. Until I was thirteen, when Lucia and I travelled out of the city for the first time, I had never seen real darkness.

I was dead tired. I had spent two months of school holidays hanging around the housing complex, some days I just put one foot in front of the other, I just lay on the couch and watched TV, and when they opened the first supermarket I went up and down the aisles on my inline skates for hours.

I felt sick on and off from hunger and fatigue, and when I closed my eyes, my head spun. Despite the fatigue, however, I was happy. The children were doing well, I had found some milk and some money. My movements were much surer than in the beginning, I could even rely on my intuition. I believed in myself and I didn't doubt that I would do the right thing.

I washed the dirty dishes and bottles. Until the children started crying again. I managed to wipe them with damp towels, put some ointment on them, I cleared the toys off the bed, and heated all the milk from the box. Adele fell asleep on my shoulder while I was carrying her around the hut so that she wouldn't choke, then I rocked Jacob on my knees. I set the alarm clock for ten, snuggled up to the warm, sleeping children, covered myself with a blanket, thanked God for letting us get through this beautiful day healthy and well, and fell into a deep sleep in less than a minute.

I awoke before ten to some noise outside. I turned off the alarm clock and went outside where I saw the tail of a white cat on the grass by the fence. It was raining. I went back inside, pulled a chair and the cardboard box up to the bed and put some pillows on the ground just in case the children fell. They were sleeping soundly, and not twitching or turning anymore. It was strange to see them so unmoving. Their arms were thrown over the blanket, their fingers spread out like flower petals. But I didn't have time to look at them, I needed to get to the 24-hour supermarket, buy milk, nappies and some food for myself and make the last tram back before they woke up.

I took the money, locked up and without even blinking flew down the hill by memory, between the garages and through the shortcut over the tracks to the tram stop. I just made it down to the tram and I didn't have any change, only the 100-note from the old woman, so, I got on the tram without a ticket.

With relief I sat down in a seat, leant my forehead on the cold window and watched the droplets running in crooked streams down the glass. When I had caught my breath and started to notice not only my hunger but also my surroundings, I spied little Christian, the boy from the building opposite ours, sitting white as a sheet in the first seat behind the driver.

I knew right away that something was wrong because Christian was never allowed to take municipal transport by himself and never stayed outside after dark. He was too trusting and careless and everyone knew it. His mother so anxiously protected him from anything bad that Christian had practically no chance to feel cold, hunger, never ever experienced the darkest darkness, has never seen violence on TV or poked a dead dog with a stick. What scared him came only from inside.

Christian was truly pale and small, shrunken as if he wanted to fit into the gap under the seat and ride around without anyone seeing him. I sat down behind him on a double seat, trying not to be noticed, and observed him for a little while.

Christian, I said as quietly and softly as I could, and Christian stiffened and started to stammer and stutter something, but no words came out, just oh, oh, I, I, I. I put my hand on his shoulder. It's me, Jarka . . . Christian, don't worry, it's me.

Christian got even smaller, curled up into himself and pulled his head down between his shoulders. I pulled him up by his T-shirt and sat him next to me on the seat.

Sit up straight and act natural, or they'll catch us, I whispered to him in a normal way and Christian suddenly shot up like a spring. I considered this a confirmation of my suspicion that he had just run away from home for the first time.

Where are you going? I don't know. Don't sniff, Christian, or you'll look suspicious. He grew even paler as he tried not to cry and to hold the horror of his actions inside. I recognized children on the run. They tried so hard to be invisible that it fairly screamed.

Come with me, we'll think of something, I whispered to him and grabbed his hand. He pulled away but only symbolically, he was after all a little boy, and even if he was younger and scared to death, the switch had been thrown in his head—the one that told him not to touch, never ever to touch a girl! Not yet, it wasn't so bad yet.

Then we were quiet the whole way and I felt how fear and doubt were slowly relaxing their grip on Christian. He was no longer alone.

Children are small and live too close to the earth, and much good remains in them from this. For children, everything is big, everything is important. They've not heard about the universe yet, they can't compare anything to its endlessness. They have clean souls, soft and fragile like paper made of silk. No one can squeeze them too hard, or they'll be crushed. No one can stuff their own truth, wishes or failures into children, because they'll rip apart and all the betrayals will tumble out at once.

They carry fear and shame inside them, many different fears, about which we know nothing anymore. We cannot imagine their depth, we've forgotten about them, rid ourselves of them. They seem banal. We laugh at them. You're a scaredy-cat aren't you! Silly goose!

I didn't ask Christian why he ran away. He would tell me himself, when he felt safer. We got off in front of the 24-hour supermarket where there were so many people that it was very easy to lose ourselves among them and not call any attention to ourselves.

Christian followed me around like a dog. Terrified by all the people he didn't know, by the street where he couldn't find his way in the dark and that he wasn't used to, by the lights that blinded him, by the plenitude of products in the supermarket that he had never been to before because his parents didn't want to burden him. He was tired because at home he went to bed at eight o'clock, exactly at eight o' clock, so that his seven-year-old body didn't get out of balance. He was terrified by his own radical decision and by his unknown future. In the line by the baskets, he took hold of my jacket, so as not to lose me, because I was his only beacon in this monstrous structure.

We had to hurry to catch the tram. Christian was out of it, I couldn't count on him very much, just lead him through the aisles and put things into the basket.

In the children's section I found milk, many different kinds, too many different kinds. The problem was that I couldn't buy a lot for my 100-note. So I stuffed one pack of nappies into Christian's empty backpack, I pulled one package of powdered milk from a box and stuffed it under my jacket. I put groceries for the two of us in the basket. Christian didn't protest, didn't say anything at all, just obediently did whatever I told him, like a robot.

When you're by the cashier's start crying, OK? I told him. Are you listening, Christian? Start to wail like crazy or they'll catch us. I'll explain everything to you afterwards. Now it's important for you to make a real scene. Think of something. Your tummy hurts, or you have to pee or something like that. The best is if you say you have to go to the bathroom. If you do what I tell you, nothing will happen to you and you'll get a good dinner too. I'm sure you haven't eaten anything since lunch. How long since you left home?

I don't know, I guess at two o'clock, mumbled the boy barely audibly, his chin beginning to tremble.

Not yet, Christian, I'll tell you when to start, OK? Do you understand? Now walk with me and smile. Be careful not to knock anything over.

In front of the cashier's there were lots of people just standing there waiting and digging in their wallets. When there was only one woman standing in front of us, I stepped on Christian's foot and first he started to carefully and purposefully sniff, then after a moment he began to bawl. Outside I had to stick a roll in his mouth to get him to stop wailing.

At eleven we were already sitting in the tram, at eleven-thirty Christian began to doubt as we moved among the garages that he wanted to sleep in a garden hut somewhere outside the city. With me—because I hadn't told him yet about the babies. So that it would be a surprise.

And where will you go Christian? What do you think your father will do if you go home now? You can't go home now . . . I told him. I needed to convince him to come with me, because in the meantime I had thought of all the things this pathetic little boy could help me with. Even if he was thus far just wandering around tripping on every stone, sobbing and sniffing, he did have two hands and two feet. When he came around, calmed down and ate something, he might be capable of checking out the other huts and snagging some food, he could watch the children and push them around the garden in the carriage. At the end of the day, he didn't have anywhere to go anyway. The rainy night-time city would devour him in an hour.

The last few metres I dragged Christian behind me like a toy train on a string. Behind us we had the dimming city, in front of us darkness. The city shone fuzzily through the mist that was lit up by the streetlamps. Like this, from afar, it was beautiful, inviting. It could have been made of chocolate and marzipan, but it wasn't. It was smeared with mud, garbage and footprints, tied together with threads of roads and railroad tracks.

Christian was frightened by the city, but the darkness outside the city, which bore down on his forehead, was even more terrifying.

Don't be afraid, my little one, I said to him, only a few more metres and we're home. Home where? You'll see.

The garden gate was squeezed between the wet branches of the hedge, it creaked and the wires that were sticking out caught his leg. Christian made a choking gasp and grabbed my hand. His fingers were as cold and rough as the iron railing in front of our school. With relief I realized that the babies weren't crying.

We went inside. I threw a T-shirt over the lamp so the light wouldn't be too bright and sat Christian down at the table. He didn't notice the sleeping children tangled in the blankets, I had the impression that he wasn't noticing anything, just sitting and waiting for the real live Bogeyman who they used to talk about to scare the children in his class.

Eat, Christian, I said to him kindly and handed him a roll and the Nutella. I felt sorry for him. A little tyke drowning in his big jacket with the sleeves hanging down over his pin-pricked fingers. A boy from a good family who was not allowed to be friends with half the housing complex. Including me and the boys with whom he'd been jumping up and down this morning like a battery-operated rabbit. A boy who'd done something bad. I stroked his head, but then something choked him. He coughed. I had to whack him on the back before it passed.

In the bed, Jacob twitched and whimpered. Psst, I whispered and revealed my two secrets, so happy that the moment to show them to Christian had arrived.

They're sleeping, I said. Aren't they beautiful? Aren't they gorgeous? This is Jacob and this is Adele.

Whose . . . whose children are those? he asked. Mine, I said. What do you mean yours? Mine. Mine, period. You have to be quiet so they don't wake up, OK? They still have to sleep longer and then we can play with them. Now we should go outside, OK, Christian?

I took the torch, the little rug and some thin slices of bread with a centimetre-thick layer of Nutella on them and pushed Christian out the door. We sat down in the doorway, hugging our knees. It was raining. Drops were falling onto the corrugated tin roof and the sound helped us breath in the same rhythm and slowly get used to each other. Now Christian wasn't shaking anymore, he freed his hands from his sleeves, leant his head back against the door and chewed vehemently.

So what happened? What did you do?

He swallowed loudly. I took Daddy's money. A thousand. They made me. Who? The guys . . . Christian started sniffing again . . . Which guys? The ones from the stadium. They said if I didn't bring it to them, they'd tell my parents that I was the one who hit Pepo with that piece of wood. I'm not allowed to fight . . . Mama said, she's always telling me . . . he started to sob suddenly . . . she's always saying the same thing, not to fight, not to be like the others, but to be good, to be good and not embarrass them. But I couldn't even fight if I wanted to, I myself, you know how many of them were there, and they were all standing over me, Pepo too and his whole face was bloody and his jacket too and his hands and they said that I have to bring the money, to the station at three, otherwise they'd go to my parents and tell them everything. He wiped himself on my shirt, look!

As he had begun suddenly, he now closed him mouth and stopped. On his T-shirt was a blurred, dark brown stain. It could have been chocolate.

Drops of rain fell uninterrupted on the grass, the stones, the roof, on our legs since we couldn't fit them under the eaves of the roof. Neither Christian's voice, nor his silence could throw them off their regular rhythm. Christian stuffed his face with bread crusts and chewed for a long time with his eyes closed. He didn't even have to continue. But it wasn't meant to be—as soon as he finished chewing, he talked on. He had taken his father's money. Before that he had never even taken one coin that he found in the gap between the parquet floorboards. A purple 1,000-note. Without permission. He went to the station, but at the last moment he got scared and got on the first tram that took him far away from his parents and the big boys. He rode the tram, got off one and got onto another, wandered around the city and then got back on the tram again and was there until I found him. He had nothing in his backpack, only his jacket and one lone banknote. His mama had definitely set it aside to buy him a new pencil case and tracksuit . . . and he took it from the bar, from the box where his father kept his unfinished cigars.

I started laughing. I laughed until I shook. So I had forced him to steal nappies in the store while he was carrying a 1,000-note in his backpack. In the morning he had still been mama's little darling and by evening he had two thefts behind him. We could have bought a grilled chicken, cola, chips, toys for the children, whatever kind of milk we wanted, even two or three boxes of it, it occurred to me. I laughed, I couldn't stop. Christian burst into tears. Don't cry, Christian, you dummy! Why didn't you tell me earlier, you wouldn't have had to steal the second time! You little idiot, I said to him and nudge his shoulder. But don't worry, they won't find you here. When it's raining, no one comes up here. When it's over? Then we'll see. Come on, let's go lie down.

And . . . Are they really yours? Christian asked naively, standing over the bed. Yes, I said. Mine. I didn't know . . . he said apologetically. He's waking up. What can I do?

At the sight of the children, the little runaway had stopped thinking about himself and calmly offered me help. He stopped sniffing, took off his jacket, hung it on a chair and stroked Adele's cheek. He touched her cautiously like a model car in a shop window. She's cold, he said. I'll stoke the wood stove, I answered. I'll stoke the fire and you rock her, he said. You know how to start a fire? I couldn't believe it. Yes. Was in the scouts, for a month. Then I fell off a rock, Mama didn't let me go anymore and . . . Good, good, I said, not letting him finish. Here's the wood, here's the kindling, the newspaper is there. You'll find the matches on the shelf. Or here, take this lighter. Do you know how to use a lighter? I don't . . . he said in shame. That's OK Christian. Maybe it will catch from the embers, try to stick some paper in first, I gave him these instructions and left him to it.

The little girl was cold and wet, her wet nappy was also cold as well as her footsie pyjamas and the sheet. I looked for something to change her into, but everything that she had with her in the bag was wet already, forgotten and kicked under the bed. I sent Christian to wash the clothes that were under the bed. I made Adele some milk. The empty box had remained in the shop, so once again I didn't know how much powder to use. But there was enough powder now and I made it so thick that it barely flowed through the hole in the nipple. When Adele drank, I wrapped her in a blanket and gave her to Christian to carry around until she burped. I pulled a string down above the wood stove and hung the wet footsy pyjamas and the things that Christian had washed. Big drops of water fell from them, because Christian didn't have the strength in his hands to wring them out, so I had to take them down again and wring them out outside. In the meantime, Christian walked around the small room leaning back like a bow. He held the child in his arms like a log.

At twelve-thirty, Jacob woke up. Nappy, milk, rock, put down. At one, Christian fell over, and with a half-finished word in his mouth, fell asleep on a chair. I threw the jacket over my shoulders and went out into the rain. It occurred to me that I should somehow drag the carriage into the hut and put the sleeping children in it, so that the two of us would also have somewhere to sleep. The pram was full of water because

I had put the piece of corrugated metal on it so badly that all the water had flowed down into it. So I poured the wood and kindling out of the big cardboard box and lined it with a thick blanket. I dressed Adele in the last dry footsies and put her down with Jacob in the box. With great embarrassment, Christian lay down next to me on the bed. It was warm and stuffy in the room because the larger logs were still smouldering.

I told Peter all of this at the end of May, on the way back from a wedding. We stopped just beyond a village, left the car on the side of the road, a few metres beyond the last house. Peter took a blanket and a bottle of water from the car. We didn't want to go far and so we walked for a while along a fence until we saw a lone apple tree on the edge of a meadow. The sky was cloudy and it was threatening to rain. Peter took a long time choosing where to put the blanket down in the broad green space. There was tall grass growing everywhere and some bluebells here and there. You could smell the distant rain in the air and hear the buzz of electricity pulsing between the high-voltage towers.

We lay tangled together in one warm cocoon and breathed nose to nose. Then he lay behind me and cuddled up to me, burying his nose in my hair. We were like two spoons in the silverware drawer. I felt his breath on the nape of my neck.

After a while, it felt like I was twelve again, it wasn't Peter lying behind me but little Christian. I felt that same feeling of warmth, peace and intimacy. I started to talk out of the blue. I told him everything about the children, the garden and Christian.

First, I talked about the boats. About the wooden boats that looked like something out of a cartoon where anything can happen. They were like skeletons and made from thickly cut boards. The gaps between the ribs of the hull have been filled in with putty and all the irregularities are covered by a layer of cobalt-blue or white paint. They seem fragile and unstable, but affable. Sometimes they have a small cabin where you can hide, sometimes they're just empty shells without oars or lines. They rock on the surface in the stagnant water without current, without wind. When I wake up, I'm sweaty and tired, and my arms hurt, as if I've been swimming or rowing all night long. I awaken disappointed and unfulfilled, feeling like I've expended a lot of energy but achieved nothing, neither the bottom, nor the port. The undercurrents haven't caught me and the wind is swirling, imprisoned in some valley far from the water.

I spoke calmly, as if I were reading, I had no idea whether Peter was listening or had fallen asleep. He didn't move, he was breathing regularly. With each word said out loud, I felt lighter and lighter. I had the feeling I was overflowing like a river at its delta, and all that turbid water that had been pulling me down towards the ground for almost twenty years could now finally be soaked up into the soil or run off into the sea.

I had never spoken continuously for so long before. No one had been willing to listen to me for so long before. In places I felt that my voice was coming from an unmoving mouth, from a closed mouth, by itself, without help from my brain, language or pens. Without resistance, without barriers, it flowed like blood from an open wound and it didn't bother me at all that I had no power over it. It wasn't even my voice anymore. Peter didn't stop me and didn't ask me anything. At a certain moment I took his hands in mine, just as I had done with Christian's small, cold hands. He didn't resist.

And Christian hadn't resisted either. He was sleeping. He lay with his back pressed to wall, curled up and helpless. He couldn't fall asleep for a long time, he tossed and murmured to himself until his fingers just happened to become entangled in my hair. That's how he used to fall asleep at home. With his mama's hair in his hands. When he felt hair between his fingers, he fell asleep in about two seconds and so deeply that his lips grew slack and saliva flowed from his half-open mouth. I untangled his fingers from my hair and took his hands again in mine. They were cold and rough—as cold as they'd been outside by the gate when the wires that were sticking out caught him and he grabbed me in terror. The skin on his fingers, especially the fingers of his left hand, were scratched and wounded. His nails were bitten down to the quick, so rough and ragged that you could have sharpened pencils on them. It was unpleasant to touch such damaged, living hands, but I felt the need to warm him up, to stroke him and show him some compassion. Poor little Christian.

He was a good boy who had to be good and obedient in every situation. Turn the other cheek and repay evil with kindness. Don't fight with the others, you won't find anyone weaker anyway. You'll always get it from someone. Stand up straight, you'll look older. Don't embarrass us. Be a good boy. Christianko.

I fell asleep, blowing hot air on Christian's hands. On the table behind my back sat a cardboard box with two sleeping children in it.

I had a vivid dream. Again, a dream with a boat and a swimming pool. Except that instead of leaves, there were drops of rain falling onto the surface of the water, and they were so big that when they hit they formed bubbles. The swimming pool looked like a big pot full of bubbling, boiling water. I'm standing in the middle, my toes barely touching the bottom, I have to tilt my head up to breathe with my nose.

The raindrops are hitting me in the eyes. Drip, drip, drip.

Hitting my forehead. Drip, drip, drip.

Hitting the water. Drip, drip, drip.

They are bouncing off the metal roofs of the changing rooms and four small boats that are drifting in the distance. I hear the muffled drip, drip, drip under the surface too. Around my neck is a string with the key to the garden on it.

The swimming pool is huge, the boats are small and far away, as if they were made of nutshells. In one of them stands Peter. In the other sits Lucia, in the third lies Irena and the fourth, it seems, is empty. Peter stands erect, his feet set wide apart like the pillar of a bridge, and loudly encourages me not to be afraid, to push off the bottom and swim to him. I hesitate. The relentless dripping and drops splattering on all sides annoying and deafening me. They won't let me concentrate on the simple movements needed for a person to get off the ground, let himself be carried by water, pulled by the current.

When I finally lift my legs, spread my arms and take a deep breath before the first stroke, Lucia, crouching in the boat, rises and speaks my name. Urgently and loudly she says, Jarka! And stretches her arms out to me. Her arms are weak and shaking under the burden of the drops. Jarka, come to me, she says again. Save me! She whispers.

At that moment, Irena, lying in the third boat with her head leaning against the bench and one arm hanging over the side, rises wheezing. The tendons in her neck stick out like the ropes. Jarka, rub my back until it's dry, she says in a gurgling voice and her head falls back onto the hard bench.

At that moment, the cries of three children sound from the fourth boat, the unbridled screaming of the two little babies and Christian's barely controlled sobbing. They are lying on the bottom of the hull, hidden under the benches.

I look around, searching for the fifth boat which would be truly empty, a boat ready for me, with a cabin complete with a solid door and latch, a door that my garden-gate key opens. In this dream though, the fifth boat hasn't sailed.

Swim! Everyone is shouting at me. Come to me, swim, wash my hair, help me, swim, calm me down, rock me, listen to me, be good, take care of us, after all, you are grown up. Drip, drip, drip. Drip, drip, drip. The little boats get bigger and closer. Lucia is standing, Irena has sat up and I see her ridiculous swimsuit. Drip, drip, drip. Christian is trying to keep his balance and pick up the two screaming babies. Peter jumps into the water and swims towards me but doesn't get any closer.

I close my eyes. I go under. I let my arms go free, still prepared to roil the water. I relax my legs as well, open my mouth. I let the water flow into my body.

A sobbing Christian woke me up. He was sitting on the corner of the bed, wiping his eyes on his sleeve and pulling on my leg. It took me a moment until I realized that both children were crying, that the whole hut was shaking with their monstrous screaming. At first, I heard only Christian's choked sobs. He was terrified and disoriented, as if he had no idea where he was or what he was doing there. He wasn't able to get out of bed by himself and quiet them, he just sat there sobbing. Wake up Jarka, wake up, he kept saying over and over pulling on my leg. I kicked him with all my might to make him stop. It was cold in the room, the fire had gone out long ago. It was four-thirty in the morning.

Jacob was calmer, he probably only woke up because Adele was crying, so I gave him to Christian to take care of. I took Adele in my arms, walked with her around the room, bounced her, sang to her. She peed on herself. Pooped on herself. Everything was wet and stinky again, the nappy, the footsies, my sweatshirt. I changed her, gave her a new nappy. With true self-denial and arms stretched out in front of me. I didn't manage to resurrect the fire fast enough, so I gave her some cold milk to drink.

Christian managed to haul the boy onto the bed. He sat down in the corner, put the baby on his knees like a log and rocked him until both of them fell asleep. I lay Christian down on the bed and put Jacob next to him. I had to carry and rock Adele. My head hurt from fatigue, yet I had no choice but to walk. Three steps to the wood stove, three steps to the bed and back again, because as soon as I stopped, Adele began to twist and whimper again. I thought I would lose my mind.

As I walked, I was falling asleep on my feet, my eyes closed, I bumped into the furniture and almost let the girl fall to the ground two or three times. I envied both boys their deep sleep. Christian was curled up into a ball with his arm around the warm little larva next to him. I covered them with a blanket, and when Adele had calmed down a little, I put her back down in the box. I sat down on a chair and with my head on the table and fell asleep as well.

At six, the merry-go-round started up again. The room was flooded in rose-coloured light, everything inside shown and sparkled, the mugs, silverware, the jar of Nutella, the bottles. The light was bright and one could suddenly see all the imperfections on the window, the bubbles in the glass, smears, fingerprints, cobwebs. If it hadn't been for those stunning rays that promised another beautiful August day, I would have run away and left all three children in the hands of fate.

I remembered how once, two or three years ago, I had woken up in the morning in some unknown room in an unknown city. I was probably ten years old.

The room had only one long, narrow window which couldn't be opened and was so close to ground level that grass was growing on the outer windowsill. I woke up and saw a room flooded with the same pink light. On the walls, the shadows of plants trembled. There was furniture and lots of clothes hanging from chairs, musical instruments leaning against the wall, everything was pink and sparkling, floating in a pink mist. For me it was a beautiful dream because I had fallen asleep at home in my bed, angry with Lucia and her noisy friends who had turned our flat into a rehearsal room for several days. So, I once again calmly closed my eyes and fell back into sleep. The last thing I saw through my half-closed eyes were two shining cymbals on the wall, two suns, and two golden coins.

I woke up about an hour later. I was in a totally ordinary coatroom in the basement space of some arts-performance hall. In the coatroom full of people who were getting changed after a concert and smelt of sweat, they were finishing half-empty bottles and packing up their instruments, and among them a drunken Lucia circulated. I was totally stiff because I'd been sleeping in a bass-violin case. The pink dream evaporated, dissolving into a godless reality.

We lived through a horrible two hours. I don't know how Christian felt when, after less than four hours of sleep, he found himself in a garden hut flooded with that strange sugar soup, but I had the feeling that he had gone into autopilot and was following orders like a robot. He was pale with circles under his eyes, and during the breaks between individual tasks, he just stood stiffly in the corner, rubbing the tips of his fingers over the wall of the stove and waited for the Bogeyman to come for him. I didn't need another child, I needed help. So, I sent him outside to get some air, run around the garden, pee and wash himself in cold water, and if it helped, he could even climb a tree, for example.

Overnight Jacob's face had taken on a strange red colour which I noticed only when daylight hit the room. Around his mouth was a small red rash, his cheeks were blotchy and his eyes swollen. I had never seen anything like it before.

While I was making a fire in the wood stove, Christian did everything I told him to. Literally. He ran through the wet grass in his Chinese canvas sneakers, peed and washed himself. He tried to brush his teeth with his finger. His mama definitely didn't let him out without brushing his teeth. He climbed up into a tree, fell out of it and scratched his calf such that it bled. He returned to the hut sopping wet, numb and even paler than before.

You're a dummy Christian, I barked at him, I hope you don't think I'm going to take care of you too! Little idiot! You should have stayed home with your mama!

Christian burst into tears. From the bed Adele began to cry too. In the box, Jacob was trying to turn onto his stomach, and when he couldn't, he wiggled unhappily.

Christian cried standing up, with his knees slightly bent, his arms frozen in an unfinished movement. His fingers looked like claws and there was blood smeared on his calf. He cried and cried until he choked, his face contorted, his entire body trembling and his claw-like hands raking the air looking for something to grab onto. He was getting on my nerves and I would rather have sent him back where I had found him the evening before, to the tram, to the depot.

I couldn't imagine then how terrified he was, how afraid he was of me, his mama, the screaming babies, the garden. I couldn't relate to him, I didn't have the energy, I was dead tired and needed to take care of the children.

I wanted to play with them, carry them into the garden, watch them, enjoy them. Take off my tennis shoes and walk through the wet grass. Eat two pieces of bread with Nutella. Eat the blackberries. I wanted to get some more information from Christian about his escape. Get something about his parents out of him, after all they had always seemed so strange to me. I wanted to just gossip a bit, wait for the announcements that reached the garden from the railway station. Watch the children sleeping

I didn't feel like listening to Christian's whining and directing his every move. I didn't feel like going around the hut and shaking off Adele's spit-up. This is not the way I had imagined it would be. I asked myself how it was possible for everything to turn like that, where had I gone wrong to make the children so unhappy? I gave them food, stole for them. I changed their nappies, rocked and entertained them. I had saved Christian from the night city, let him sleep in my bed. Hidden him from his parents. So where did I go wrong?

Stop it Christian, stop wailing! I screamed at him, grabbing him by the shoulders and shaking him. Stop already . . . you little brat . . . I said again and took him by the hand. He was terribly cold. I wanted to shake him hard again and send him outside, so I could have some peace, but instead I hugged him, buried my nose in his wet hair and squeezed him like my third child. Something inside me broke. As if I'd gone through the narrow neck of a bottle full of darkness.

I burst out crying. Poor Christian, I whispered, poor little boy. Good boy . . . everything's going to be OK, everything's going to be OK . . . I said more to myself than to him, watching through Christian's mussed hair the red face of the boy in the cardboard box. Christian shook, his teeth were chattering, and I was not convincing enough for him to relax and believe that the situation we found ourselves in was still normal.

The baby's red face didn't help either. That red blotchy face shone like a red flag marking a critical point on the horizon. The place beyond which the land cracks, heaves and collapses into the earth.

The stalks of grass beyond the window sparkled and swayed in the wind, and I imagined how the grass rustles and the rain droplets burst in the air, when a cat runs through the garden. The rain started again and drops fell on the metal roof with new strength. It was like something fizzing and those were the individual drops. Not warning signs, not avalanches. Just grass and rain. Nothing more.

Everything will be OK, Christian. Everything will be OK I said to him then, as the bottle of darkness tipped over and I once again found myself in the daylight. Now take off your clothes and put on my sweater, under the bed there's a plastic bag with some old clothes in it, find something in it for yourself. It doesn't matter what you put on, no one will see you here. Quickly, before you catch cold. Hurry up!

I turned on the extra generator. I changed both children's nappies, quickly and skilfully. I managed to interest Adele in a plastic cup from the railway-station coffee machine, and Jacob in the wrinkled apple hanging from the string. I fed the babies again, carried Adele around the hut again until she burped. I spilt a little dried milk. I wiped the floor. I put out the fire because the room was becoming unpleasantly stuffy. We each ate two pieces of bread with Nutella and a bowl of blackberries.

Outside the grass was genuinely rustling. Just as I had imagined it. The wet stalks were glued to each other and moving under the weight of the raindrops. Water dripped from the blackberries. An apple fell from the tree. Somewhere in the distance an ambulance siren could be heard. One of the refinery's smokestacks was still burning. The city lived, but at a completely different tempo from the garden. No one down there knew about the four children hidden behind the hedge.

No one knew about us and I liked that very much. I was starting to like this game of functioning family again.

I put the blackberries into my inside-out T-shirt and sat down under a tree on one of the big wandering stones. Yesterday it wasn't there, today it was. In a place where the earth was almost dry, under the crown of the apple tree, set up like a throne. I was pleased again and, it could be said, even happy.

The only thing that bothered me a bit and disrupted the life of our family was the little boy's face, its colour and swelling, which didn't bode well. I calmed myself with the fact that the boy wasn't crying anymore or less than the day before and apparently nothing hurt him. And if nothing hurt him, then everything was alright, and the red would definitely go away by itself just the way it had appeared.

I didn't know anything then about reflux or allergies, about the anaphylactic shock that can happen after ingestion of allergens. I was healthy, I usually got over colds and only went to the hospital when Lucia urgently needed to get rid of me for a few days. She would claim that I had severe headaches and fainting spells so that they would keep me under observation. I got out of going to school and she could travel for business. It wasn't bad in the hospital, there were hot meals and long slippery corridors. Lucia always brought some pretty good presents from her trips so it didn't bother me that much. When my paediatrician didn't want to send me to any specialists because she knew I was healthy, Lucia found me another doctor.

I didn't know that babies were so fragile inside. Like the mechanisms inside wristwatches whose cogs fit precisely together and one broken tooth in the wheel or one rusty part could throw the whole thing off. One nut was enough.

What would you do if Jacob cried a lot, bled or coughed? Peter asked me one day. I would have taken him to the hospital and left him with all his stuff in the waiting room.

What would you do if Jacob didn't wake up in the morning? If his red face meant that he was dead?

What would I do? And what would you do? What could any a ten-year-old child do at a moment like this?

I looked through the window at what Christian was doing. He had grown livelier, woken up, and was behaving as if he'd eaten some magic beans. He wanted to do everything himself. He wanted to change the children, dress them, carry them around and feed them. He wanted to start the fire, which we didn't need at the moment, and chop wood to replace what we had used. He became talkative, commented on everything. He continually stroked the children on their hands and heads, hugged them and made faces at them. He talked to them as adults would. Gaga-googoo-gaga. He lisped and used almost exclusively diminutive, endearing language, swallowed his syllables and made everything softer. He spent more time with Jacob, perhaps because he was a boy, perhaps because Jacob's face had taken on the colour and form that it had.

People definitely do not avoid looking at anything abnormal and children do it in a wonderfully direct way. Children just stop and stare. At missing limbs, a patch over the eye, an ugly face. Christian positively enjoyed it, he looked at the boy up close, nose to nose, touching him softly, wiping him with a napkin when he drooled. It made an impression, the awkwardness and awe that showed on his face, his attempt to take care of the children and not deal with his own problems.

He was sweet and attentive, always fixing something and cleaning up. The folds in the blanket, the light, the toys. He was like a well-brought-up domestic helper doing things in a certain mechanical way that he had observed in the world of adults. A child who has understood too soon that outward appearances are important and, thus, has suppressed his own natural way of being. It wasn't difficult to imagine him at home in their sitting room—a sitting room with a circular dining table that seated eight in a concrete apartment block of flats, no one believed him when he said they actually had one and used it—sitting with his hands on his knees opposite his mama waiting for instructions. When the order sounded, Christian put his elbow on the table and took the spoon in his hand, wiped his mouth with a napkin and brushed crumbs into his hand. At home he definitely cleaned up his toys before going to bed and when he came home from school, he changed into sweatpants and a T-shirt. Since he was little, he'd been rinsing his mouth with mouthwash and when Mama told him to close his eyes and go to sleep, he closed his eyes and fell asleep.

At first glance, Christian's mama was almost perfect, well-groomed, always colour-coordinated, nothing looked off about her, nothing was provocative. She was so perfect that it drove you crazy. It wasn't hard to imagine how his mama would take Christian to see the child psychologist. He walks next to her, quiet and stiff and tries not to call attention to himself and not to make any noise or shade. He tries to be a good and happy little boy. Not to disappoint Mama. Not to be the cause of her migraine. Like all children. On the way there, Mama smiles at everyone, so that no one would guess their destination. He didn't go to our school psychologist but to one in a neighbouring city. Despite this, everyone knew. Christian's mama consulted every event in her son's life with experts, the pins and the totally banal fights and arguments. Every adverse comment by a teacher was followed by a trip to the school and a detailed investigation. The children laughed at him, Christian is a wacko, Christian is psycho. Christian, stick your head in the toilet and tell the doctor what you saw down there. Christian is gay, Christian peed in his pants.

Mama will definitely get divorced now, he said suddenly when all four of us were lying on the bed playing.

Why would she get a divorce? Because she said that if I'm bad, Father will leave us and they'll get a divorce. He'll leave because of me.

Why would he leave because of you? Because I'm bad. I stole. And lied.

It's normal, you're not the first or the last. Dummy, do you know how many times I've stolen from the store? And what happened to me? Nothing. You're little, you'll get away with it. They'll be happy that you're home.

No, no, my parents will get divorced and put me in an orphanage. My mama said so.

When did she tell you that? She says it all the time. When I don't do what she tells me. She says they'll have to bring me up to the orphanage and leave me there.

Don't think about that, Christian, and turn Jacob over onto his stomach, you see how he's straining. I'll go and make the milk, the children will be hungry. It's already almost ten o'clock.

They'll definitely put me in an orphanage, said Christian, convinced that he was right, and turned Jacob onto his stomach. And don't say it won't happen, Jarka, he stressed one more time.

I could imagine Christian's mama live. A completely different type from Lucia. Exactly the opposite. She dreamed of a crystal-clear and precise plan for Christian's life and future. She had clarified every detail, paid attention to correct timing and didn't want to leave anything to chance. She watched his every move, meddled in everything, she subtly and suggestively asked whether he wasn't thirsty or tired and convinced him that he should drink or lie down. She determined when and where he sat and which book he should feel like reading, chose his clothes so that they matched. She cooked him healthy food. He only got cake as a reward. Half a piece so that he wouldn't have cavities. Made of organic flour, so that he wouldn't have toxins in his body. She didn't trust his judgement, didn't believe that he was clever enough to guess by himself what he should do when. She was afraid for him, afraid he wouldn't survive without her guidance. She still put him, a school-age child, to bed so she could check his breathing and body temperature during the night. He couldn't fall asleep by himself, only with his hand in her hair. She had only him and couldn't look forward to any more children, because her husband didn't desire any more. Her husband didn't want it, because children are expensive, noisy and get under your feet.

The children continually required our attention and Christian strove with all his might to be a proper father. He was clumsy, and there were some tools he didn't know how to use because at home he was never allowed to do anything dangerous. Like use a knife or sharp scissors, browse the Internet, climb trees or ride a bicycle without a helmet. In the garden hut almost everything was dangerous, from the amateurishly installed electricity to the mouse droppings in the tea mugs. Edges and sharp blades threatened Christian from every corner. And new opportunities too. No one was breathing down his neck. No one was dictating to him. I was careful that he didn't do anything dumb, like burn down the hut or do cartwheels with the babies, but otherwise he was free. He could leave, he could stay. He could return home, but he didn't show any interest. Outside, there awaited a band of boys, a disappointed mama, a father ready for divorce, teachers who could give him a bad grade for conduct and tens of cruel children just waiting for him to make a false move. In the garden, he was covered—he had food and entertainment taken care of.

And the two babies too! He could examine them, feel their bodies, look into Adele's nappy. He'd never seen anything like that in his life.

In the morning, his 'mama' would pack egg-salad sandwiches and granola bars in his backpack and generously let him go out for two hours. She even let him go beyond the road, out there, further than the eye could see; she let him truly enjoy his last week of holiday to the fullest. And in the evening, instead of being put to bed at eight o'clock in an aired out room after a good dinner, he had to wash poopy baby footsies in the dark, in the rain, completely alone, and reconcile himself to the fact that he had stolen from his parents.

I heard about two stepsiblings who fell so much in love with each other that they decided to get married. The girl was seven and the boy six. As a witness, they took their five-year-old sister with them. On the morning of New Year's Day, before their parents had woken up, they took the tram to the railway station. There, they planned to get on a train and go to the airport. In their suitcases they had packed food, bathing suits and inflatable toys because they were headed for Africa. After all, in Africa it was warm and sunny.

I heard about two friends who ran away from school, riding 3 kilometres across the city on scooters. They found them in a supermarket in the toy aisle.

I read about two twelve-year-olds from Tuscany whose parents didn't want them to see each other. The children used their savings to go to Venice. Hand in hand, they strolled the stone streets, stopped on the bridges, and when night came, they entered an appealing small pensione where they asked for a room. The receptionist understood what these children were experiencing. He called the police and they took the children on a gondola ride and showed them the entire city by boat. Only then did they take them to a former monastery in the precinct. There the children spent the night in separate rooms and the next day, in a room with a view of a fifteenth-century courtyard, they were set a table and offered a three-course lunch. Then the parents arrived, and the romance was gone.

I know children who run away regularly, two or three times a month, but at the last minute, they always come back. No one understood their attempts at escape. It looked like ordinary disobedience, like getting lost while walking the dog, or taking the wrong tram on the way back from school, for which they'd be grounded for two days. I know children who've made it across the border, and some who were never found again. Running away would have definitely done Christian good. If he hadn't happened to meet me on the way.

When we were lying in bed, Christian on one side and I on the other with the children between us, I didn't see anything else but those little hands trying to catch the apple hanging on the string, the little legs in constant motion, the bulging bellies and folds on Jacob's face. I heard only their babbling, Christian's affected comments and the diminutives he incorporated into them, and the rain, the waterfall constantly falling on the roof. Everything else faded into the distance, as if the garden had broken off from the shore and floated into a sea of joy and forgetting like a lonely raft.

After some years this image and the feelings that were associated with it returned. Peter and I were sitting in the car, we had got lost. The car was clawing its way up a slight incline, along a dirt road through the fields, whirls of dust and stones flying everywhere from under the wheels. He was quiet, I was quiet, but I didn't have any tense feeling of guilt like I had unwittingly created a problem and now he was letting me know by being silent. Letting me know that I'm a stupid woman who can't read a map. We simply made a mistake, he or I and at a certain moment, we had decided to go a different way. Maybe that's where the wind was blowing from, maybe there was a bell ringing in the distance.

We closed the windows so the dust wouldn't settle on the dashboard. The bushes scraped the paint on the car, the motor yowled like a dog, but nothing disturbed the peace of the pastures and wide-open spaces beyond this barely passable road. Then Peter suddenly jerked the wheel and took the car across a well-grazed meadow. He stopped at the foot of a wood, two ruts in the grass trailing behind us. We sat down on the ground, leaning up against the wheels of the hot car and looked out over the landscape. After a moment, Peter took off his shoes, lay down on his side, put his head down on my thigh and hugged my legs. His hair was already grey at the temples then, the skin on his neck a bit loose. Everything was stacked and set like a puzzle solved.

I closed my eyes and saw Christian's face, the apple swinging above the babies' heads, their hands, the spoons placed on the cooled-down stove. I opened my eyes and saw Peter, felt the weight of his body, his warmth. Objects, smells, sounds, an instant. A meeting that can't be planned. A functioning mechanism that gathers momentum quietly, and seemingly all by itself. I was complete.

The milk ran out. While I was sitting outside on the stones, Christian in his frenzy had spilt part of the powder onto the floor by mistake and, instead of telling me, had swept it under the bed and blown up the almost-empty packet and left it on the shelf. So that I wouldn't notice. This really made me angry. Such naivety. Naivety that I was already lacking and had no empathy for. I would never have expected such a thing from a boy who was able to stick pins under his own fingernails, but I told myself that I wouldn't shout at him, but he would have to correct his own mistake.

Take your money, Christian, and go find some milk, OK? Put on your clothes—they're still wet, but it doesn't matter because it's raining outside anyway. Keep my sweater on and put the hood over your head so that no one recognizes you. But everyone's sitting at home anyway, just look how it's pouring out. Here's my backpack and another bag. OK? OK. Get on the No. 5, but don't go all the way to the supermarket, that would take a long time, it's enough to go one stop and run into the small grocery shop. You know which one. Next to the pharmacy. Do you understand? Get two boxes of long-life milk, the one with the blue cow, and something to eat. I'll leave it up to you, it's your money. Buy something reasonable, so that we can eat our fill. Do you understand? And hurry up, because the children are already hungry. If it weren't for you, they wouldn't be hungry, Christian. Hurry!

I didn't let him get a word in, but just threw instructions at him, and he didn't even manage to take a breath and he already had his damp trousers hung over one arm and the backpack over the other. Without a word, he took off the big sweatpants that were rolled up three times and put on his own pants. He was shaking the whole time, but I pushed him out the door anyway. The punishment seemed fair to me.

But Christian got scared and started to resist. He wailed, ahyayahyayahhhhh I can't go, Deeeebbie, please, ooooooh . . . I don't want to, I'm not going anywhere . . . alone . . . please, please . . . and so we struggled for a moment in the doorway, he holding onto the hinges and me pushing him out with my knees.

Christian, the children are hungry, it's your fault that we have no milk. You simply have to go, I yelled.

Waaaaah . . . please, pleeeeeease . . . he wailed, but I was unbending, I had decided to send him out even if it was freezing outside, and the more he resisted, the more I was determined to close the door in his face. But Christian started to cry so piteously that I pulled him inside again so that he didn't give us away with his wailing. I grabbed him by the shoulders and shook him.

Christian, stop it. You don't want to make another scene here! We need milk because the children are hungry. So get hold of yourself and go buy some milk, and fast, OK? Hurry! Or go home and don't come back! And stop crying, the babies are scared of you, I told him, I picked Jacob up and started to deliberately walk around the room with him. I bumped into Christian on purpose so he would realize that he was in the way and should get out. Christian, however, didn't make a move to go anywhere, he just stood there shaking. I walked back and forth bumping into him.

Adele started crying. I stopped right in front of him and said to him quietly that he should truly go. The babies are hungry, can you hear that? Or do you want to stay with them here by yourself? Should I lock you in with them? With both of them? Will you take care of them? Huh? After these words, Christian gave in, took the backpack and left.

And hurry up! I shouted after him again. Through the window I saw him wading slowly through the tall grass, looking around, seeking help among the stones, in the tops of the trees.

It was ten-forty. If he didn't return in an hour, I would have to go get some milk myself. Too bad he didn't steal the money in smaller banknotes, I would have nicked two or three from him and had one less problem.

By noon the children were screaming so much that I decided to dope them up with vitamins. I mashed some washed black-berries in a dish with a spoon and guided them into their pursed mouths in small doses. One for Jarka, one for Christian, one for Adele, one for Jacob. They ate everything and what I couldn't pick up with my fingers I licked off the plate. They fell asleep and I with them.

I remember one dream from long ago. It wasn't a dream from that day, or the night before, I don't know when it snuck in, but it still sits in my head like a stone.

The housing complex in the middle of winter. New snow has fallen and I am walking along the pavement, which follows the shallow river bed. A man is leading me by the hand. I don't know who it is, I don't raise my head and look into his face. In the dream I'm about five years old, dressed in a red jacket with two blue stripes on the sleeves, on my head is a white fur cap. Two pom-poms hang from it on strings bouncing up and down on my breasts and I like them. We are walking slowly, as slowly as the snow is falling, except that sometimes I skip so that the pom-poms will swing. The snow is squeaking and only that squeaking can be heard, as if the snow had sucked up all the other sounds, the screaming children, starting cars, the river.

There's a child—a girl—walking in front of us, a little bigger than I am, pulling a sled. She's laughing, jumping, she pushes the sled, then pulls it, then she sits down on it and tries to push it forward with her legs. You can see that she's saying something to me, but I only hear the snow—I don't understand her, I cannot read anything from her lips. I'm not thinking about the man who is leading me along, my hand feels safe and natural in his big glove. I don't wonder about him, because I have the feeling that he is always somehow present in me. I am part of him and he part of me. He walks alongside me, but it seems to me like he is floating above me. He doesn't block my light or pull me. I like my white pom-poms, I think about them and turn my head so that they swing even more.

The girl suddenly starts running, stopping about 20 metres in front of us, she pushes the sled to the edge of the pavement, to where the bank slopes down to join the river, and sits down on it. She laughs, lifts her legs so high that her pants come up revealing childish calves in green tights. With all her might, she pushes off and takes off down the slope. The river foams, drops of water and pieces of shattered ice spray into the air. Then the surface closes up and the river flows on as freely and quietly as before.

We walk on, the man floats beside me, the pom-poms hit me gently in the chest and multiply the beating of my heart.

I have the impression that the girl is my sister, and the man who is leading me by the hand is my father. Maybe it's Peter. Or maybe it's someone else's dream, I've never had a father or a sister.

I remember exactly that odd feeling of being bound to the man who was leading me by the hand. My fingers fit between his like the teeth of a zipper, I don't have to look for his hand, it's waiting for me, it's exactly where I need it to be. One of his steps is equal to two of my child steps. I would go anywhere with him, into the dark, under the surface of a frothing river, anywhere.

When Peter and I were in the meadow sitting up against that muddy car, he said to me, you speak many languages. Don't talk nonsense, I answered. I don't know what languages you're talking about, I said. That's because some of them can only be spoken between a couple, he said.

It stopped raining, so I took the children outside for some fresh air. First, I poured the water out of the pram, dried it off and lined it with dry blankets. I felt like an animal preparing her den, filling it with grass and fur. I pulled the carriage under the apple tree and sat down on a stone.

The air smelt of water, the grass was fragrant, the city was far away, our raft was getting smaller, floating further away. The water was rising, flowing through the gaps into the boat from my dreams, flooding my eyes.

The children were quiet, they just lay there looking around. Jacob still had a blotchy face, but I had already grown used to his colour. Adele must have had a temperature. I took the covers off her so she would cool down. My stomach, full of Nutella, grew hard, it was tiny and it irked me, like a walnut stuffed into a too-small pocket in my pants.

The children were quiet just lying there and looking around. I was happy that they were happy.

I imagined how that day would have been if, for example, we had had a full refrigerator and I didn't have to look for forgotten food in the apartment. If I hadn't noticed that little piece of paper under Lucia's unfinished piece of bread, if I hadn't met those boys and beaten one up with a stick. If I hadn't lingered at the grocer's and if the empty drink can on the pavement in front of the railway station had hit a stone and changed directions.

What would I have done? Walked around the housing complex, the same as the day before yesterday, like the month before. I would have played hopscotch with the little kids from our building, ridden round and round on the merry-go-round. I would have sat around at bus stops, at the broken-down stadium, in front of the supermarket, on the steps, in the best of cases in the garden under the apple tree. I would have ridden into the centre of town and back again. Perhaps I would already have thought about school and looked forward to the lunches in the school cafeteria. I would have stood by the kitchen window and looked down onto the parking lot to see whether anyone was dropping Lucia off. Then I would have cooked something and eaten, alone at the big kitchen table. First some spaghetti with ketchup straight from the pot, so that I wouldn't have to wash any extra dishes. I would have watched television long into the night, some thriller or romantic comedy. I would have slept in Lucia's bed.

I used to sleep in Lucia's bed when she left me alone overnight. I felt her there, felt her warmth and her smell. In that warmth I didn't have strange dreams, only my dreams, good ones, pleasant and comprehensible. And when Lucia would come back during the night, she would usually turn on the neon light, wake me up and take me to my cold bedroom. My nice dreams and the warmth I had worked hard to accumulate she kept for herself in her bed. That was typical of her.

I waited for Christian. Under the tree, with bare feet with wet leaves stuck to them and the taste of Nutella in my mouth. The children lay in the carriage already almost fully still, like dolls. Only the motion of their eyes following everything that moved showed that they were still alive and curious, and that not only the helicopter flying low to the ground had the strength to make those eyes move but each leaf on the apple tree as well, each bird and fly.

The helicopter flew unusually low and slowly and I instinctively crouched down when the apple tree showered me with some of its leaves.

Children on the verge of puberty say that they'll never be like their parents, that they will never ever repeat that circus that their parents make every day at home. Parents think they are understanding, tolerant and free-thinking people, and want only the best for their children. With foresight, however, they count on their children appreciating this when the years have passed, when they get smarter and understand many things from their own experience. Only then, when we parents aren't here anymore . . .

They will develop healthy relationships, will be sincere and honest. They won't repeat their parents' mistakes, and in time will clear the road that lies in front of them. Clear away the debris of unfulfilled dreams, the complexes and ambitions of their parents, because they disrupt the smooth flow of the machine of love. Because it's about love, love above all. Love must be kept alive at any price and at the same level as at the beginning, its quality and depth must be carefully maintained. Love among all members of the household. Attention to detail, flowers.

They will be understanding, sensitive, they will listen and be quiet when necessary. They won't humiliate anyone and won't let anyone demean, beat or blackmail them, won't stop holding hands even after years and won't be embarrassed to kiss in public. They will talk, eat lunch together, plan and swim together and sleep together in the same room. So that neither love, nor passion is lost as the years go by, they will pay attention to their appearance and stay in shape, and they won't hold back their monogamous sexual fantasies. They won't covet their neighbours' wives or husbands.

They won't shout at their children, won't shoo them away like flies. They will answer all their questions. They won't drink so much that their children will have to drag them out of the ditch, or, no matter how small they are, be their crutch as they walk home. They will behave well, so that their children won't be afraid or ashamed to talk, laugh or cry in front of them. They will be models for their children. An ideal ornament already imagined, a copy of a map that can only be better and more perfect. Forever and ever. Amen.

Two hours had passed since Christian left. I went out onto the road, but Christian was nowhere to be seen. I saw, however, a few people, adults, walking along the furrow between two rows of vines, so I decided to return and take the children back into the house. I started a fire in the stove and boiled some water. I shook out some granules of milk powder from the folds in the packet, but it wasn't even enough for one teaspoon. So, I took the flour and mixed it into the water instead of the milk powder. The liquid looked the same and didn't taste any worse and I, pleased with my creative approach to the problem, poured one bottle each into Jacob and Adele. I was really happy with myself and the way events had progressed. The children drank the coloured water in one swoop and Adele's stomach didn't even throw it back up. They didn't cry. Adele was hot, so I put a damp cloth on her head. I wanted to change them but both were dry and so I read them an article from the newspaper that was meant for the stove. I turned them on their stomachs facing each other so they could talk a little. I put some toys down around them. I cleaned up, counted the nappies, peed. I put some quartered apples in hot water and drank the resulting tea. Again, I ran out onto the road, but didn't see Christian.

Christian came running in just before six. At first glance, it was clear that he hadn't been strolling for hours under the cherry blossoms but instead had been through something he wasn't the least bit prepared for. My nice sweatshirt was destroyed, his trousers were muddy and he was missing his left tennis shoe. Water was pouring off him, dripping onto the swept floor. He was hugging bags to his chest, his backpack was full to bulging and his face was like a suitcase, which was in itself a report on the life of its owner, banged up, covered with stickers, dirty.

Any whiff of resistance from Christian had evaporated. I could have twisted his arms behind his back or yanked on his pee-pee, and I don't think he would have even flinched. He was cold and would definitely not have won a contest for the most handsome Second Grader, but when he victoriously handed me the backpack full of food, his face beamed with pride and happiness and I had to bite my tongue so as not to ask why, for God's sake, he had taken so long.

First, he pulled out of the backpack, one at a time, fresh rolls, fish spread, hotdogs, chips, chocolate, milk for the children, rattles and two pairs of socks with little teddy bears on them, pudding-filled pastries, spaghetti, a series of model cars with a wind-up mechanism, crayons and frozen French fries. It was only after he had spread everything out on the table, that he realized he was terribly cold, and his teeth began to chatter. I took his clothes off him, carefully and without silly comments, until he stood in the middle of the room completely naked, white as a baby bird, only his calves and arms black with mud. He covered his miniature penis with his hands, but didn't protest, because my hands were no longer anything terrible in comparison with the cold, the rain and the thorn bushes and tall, wet grass and dirt. I wiped the dirt off him with the damp towel from Adele's forehead. I sat him on the bed wrapped in a blanket and gave him some apple tea to drink that was left in the bottom of the glass. I handed him some of the toy cars as well, and socks and rattles so that he could play with them himself and show the children. He ate one pastry, warmed up and calmed down. I didn't find out anything from him, except that he had sat for a long time in a hole. He fell asleep by the time I had finished cooking the spaghetti.

In the pocket of his trousers I found more than a hundred and fifty in coins and small banknotes. I hid half of it in a sock and returned the other half.

Jacob recovered a bit from his apathy, twitched, kicked his legs and took the blanket off of the sleeping Christian. The rash around his mouth had faded, or I had got so used to it that it no longer seemed strange.

Adele had a fever. When I sat her on my knee, she couldn't hold her head up straight, she was soft and limp like a stuffed bear, her arms hanging from her like two pieces of spaghetti. She was sweating, but her nappy was still dry and it didn't occur to me at all that this wasn't a good thing. I thought about how the nappy would at least last us a while. The room was overheated and the children warmly dressed. That's what they always told me, dress well, so that you don't get sick and if you've already got sick, get into bed and cover yourself with a quilt. That's why I had dressed the children in sweaters, and when they fell asleep, I had covered them with a blanket.

I didn't feel like sleeping or sitting at the table and listening to Christian sighing and smacking his lips in his sleep. I was cold and so I decided to run home and get some clothes and medicine. I went out wearing only a T-shirt because my sweatshirt was destroyed, and I borrowed Christian's backpack. I locked the children in from the outside so that no one would steal them. It was raining constantly and monotonously. The ruts criss-crossing the road had begun to deepen and fill with water running off the vineyards. The whole summer it had been dry and hot, the earth as hard as concrete. And that summer had ended today, I said to myself. Definitively. I'll have to stop at Dorota's and find out what I needed for school, she always knows about those things. I'll leave the children with Christian and go by tram tomorrow evening to the supermarket, I thought, buy some notebooks and a tracksuit, if I had enough money. And tennis shoes for Christian. Nappies for the children. Christian had forgotten to buy them, but the babies weren't using many. I probably wouldn't have enough for Christian's tennis shoes, only if I found some money in Lucia's room. And we'd have to think up something for school. It starts in four days. Four days is an eternity.

The whole day I just moved around the garden and inside the hut, and I had got so used to that world that when I needed to go down to the city, I felt nervous, as if I had to perform for parents at a school assembly. Everything looked strange: the city and its reflections in the puddles, the people wading through the mud of the vineyards in pairs, the twilight that settled slowly over the earth and with great difficulty. I ran down the hill, jumping in the puddles and making the water splash as high as possible. I ran until the garages and then, just before I reached them, I inhaled and raced through them in one breath.

The housing complex was empty, there were only about five or six people who were looking for something in the bushes that grew along the wall of the chemical plant. It seemed to me that a few figures were looking over the wall into the empty space there, but I didn't think about them after that because I had noticed that the light in our flat was on. The nervousness that had disappeared during my run returned again and made my stomach clench. Suddenly I felt intense confusion, I should have been happy that Lucia was finally home, but I had actually been looking forward to an empty flat and dry clothes, nothing more. I was thinking of the children, and Christian. I definitely didn't want to stay there long. I needed to take some things, but somehow, I couldn't get myself to come out of the shadow of the tree I was under and put the key in the entranceway door. I turned and looked at the wall of the building opposite. The light was on in Christian's father's office. The cone of light from the bulb was unmoving over the desk. Could something be deduced from this? In the end, nothing.

I was so unexcited about going inside the flat. I imagined how cold and damp it was, the most uncomfortable flat in the complex. I imagined the sleeping children and Christian tangled in the blanket and the hedge with its spikes of thorny branches sticking out. It was useless to stand around among these monstrous high-rises when I could be sleeping next to them.

I was just about to move, when I heard a quiet, frightened whistling. Two shadows unglued themselves from the building wall and ran towards me, two small figures with identical movements. Pete and Mat.

Jarka, did you hear what happened? They both blurted out at once. Christian disappeared! Do you know anything about it? The police were here too . . . they were at our house too . . . and they asked us . . . when we saw him last . . . and where . . . one talked over the other, but at the same time, as if they had practiced it, so fast that they were gasping for breath. And there are police cars around too somewhere, they circle around all the time . . . didn't you see them?

They were excited, because Christian was their friend and lived in the next entrance over from them and they were terrified, because they were at home alone waiting, and since Christian had disappeared, they might disappear too.

All the neighbours are looking for him, we're going to, said Pete conspiratorially and Mat hit him between the shoulder blades so that he wouldn't talk so much. We're going to look for our parents, Pete said, correcting himself. Haven't you seen them? added Mat as he dragged his brother away.

They'd descended on me like an avalanche and then suddenly walked away. A tramped-down line in the grass remained in their wake. I ran out of the shadow of the tree onto the pavement so I could see them hopping around the puddles. If I hadn't known that in a few minutes, maybe an hour, they'd be pulling their mama home across the grass from one of her pilgrimages, I would have said they were two happy-go-lucky and content twins who are going to the night grocer's to buy some poppy-seed cake. I always had the impression that they lived through these trips like a kind of game of hide and seek with friends, nothing strange about them, nothing tragic, a normal part of their life. The radius of their parents' activity wasn't too large and the kids could do the evening rounds of the local pubs and beer kiosks in their sleep. They knew all the spots like a postman knows his territory.

At that moment, a truck flew past, spraying me with water from the gutter. The only thing I could do was get a hold of myself and go open the door.

The light in the hall wasn't working, I felt a broken matchstick that was stuck into the switch.

I opened the door with my key and took off my shoes, but when I took the first step inside, something brushed against my leg, something rough and cold. I jumped back towards the door and turned on the light. Clothes were strewn all over the floor, sweaters and jackets and Lucia's fake furs, waist length. Warm clothes, which we always put into black garbage bags after winter was over, lining them with newspapers so that the printer's ink would ward off the moths, and stowed them in the closet. These bags now lay in the doorway to Lucia's bedroom, there was still some stuff in them, but I don't know what, because it's not wise to look into black plastic bags.

The scene of that mess was horrible, you couldn't walk between them, there was no way to get around them, and with each step something got caught on my leg. The rags and wrinkled-up newspaper meant that Lucia was home but dealing with something else.

Otherwise, the flat was empty. I looked in the refrigerator, but the sight of its contents was as pitiful as two days earlier. I looked into the bathroom, the floor was wet, the mirror sprayed with water, the soap sticky at the bottom of the sink. The chaos in Lucia's bedroom was standard, my room looked like it had been cleaned out, but it hadn't. On my pillow lay two 50-crown banknotes, some small change and an almost transparent cigarette rolling paper. On the floor a pen with a broken tip was rolling around. On the paper were two letters: DE, for Jarka, I guess. It was still sort of legible, the E already a bit rubbed off, because the pen had stopped writing. No one bothered to look for another pen and so the sentence was left unsaid. I found a second pen and wrote on the paper that Jarka was sleeping at Dorota's.

Several pieces of winter clothing had also found their way into my bedroom. A red jacket with two stripes on the sleeves, a white fur cap with pom-poms, which I knew well, and the green tights of the sledding girl from my dream, which I had never seen before in the black bags.

I changed, took the money, some T-shirts, underwear, a clean towel and several of my smaller-sized clothes for Christian. I poured all the medicines from the box and the paper instructions for them into the side pocket of my backpack.

On the street I realized that I hadn't turned out the light in the kitchen, but I wanted to leave as soon as possible and so it went out of my head. It had stopped raining and the streetlamps were reflected in the puddles. I walked on the edge of the pavement, as far from the road as possible, so that the cars wouldn't splash me, I walked quickly and straight, with my hood pulled way down over my forehead. When I spied the police in front of the night grocer's, I ran off the pavement and continued behind a building. Then I ran across about a 200-metre stretch of lit road and walked further along the dark tracks, under the bridge to the family houses and garages. I was afraid. In my stomach there was a medium-sized block of concrete. I started to feel really afraid.

On my monitor, from time to time, a window appears with text that reads, 'Please free some memory, then choose retry.' I think to myself, one couldn't say it any better.

In the sea in China, at a depth of 1,400 metres, there is a lake made of carbon dioxide. Under normal circumstances, carbon dioxide would be a gas, but deep in the ocean, under high pressure, it becomes a liquid underwater lake, a lake at the bottom of the ocean. You can see the line of it along the shore, the surface, the choppy waves, a surface beneath the surface. It takes a moment until you realize what you are actually seeing and can admit that such a thing exists.

Three children sleeping next to each other in a blue garden hut that reminds you of a steamboat. An iron stove and plates of leftover spaghetti on the table, toys, bottles, tiny model cars. My private lake under the crumbling surface of real space and time. When I looked at that still-life through the rain-washed windowpane, I couldn't believe that I was allowed to enter and find my place in this small and seemingly harmonious world. It wasn't hard to leave the housing complex, the boredom, the empty flat and unfinished note, and forget about them. It was enough to just open the door and go in.

The windowpane was criss-crossed with crooked little streams and mirrors of water drops. There, where I had leant my forehead, the network was interrupted. Under the window was the bed, the table opposite, the chair and, in the dark corner, the stove from prehistoric times. I only saw it because I knew it was there. Behind the door an air rifle stood leaning against the wall. It wasn't visible, but it too was there somewhere. There was a dirty dish remaining on the table, its golden rim shining. On the bed, only a few centimetres from me, on the other side of the wall, lay Christian and the babies. Christian was curled up. His bottom stuck out over the edge of the bed and his forehead touched the wall. From underneath the blanket, his feet were sticking out, his calves pink and soft to the eye, the ankles like scraped-up mounds. On the opposite end was his honey-coloured hair.

The children slept in Christian's embrace. Jacob wasn't visible, except for his tiny hand placed on the pillow like a jewel. Adele lay in the middle, with a half-open mouth and hair plastered down with sweat. Every now and then she twitched in her sleep and smiled. Where the children were not lying, there were toys, rattles and little cars. The weak light fell only on my face and these three children, everything else was submerged in darkness.

This memory is the only proof I have that stands between me and all the accusations. There's no way to pull it out and produce it and prove that we liked being together, that we didn't want to hurt anyone. I was never able to use it in my defence. It's just one clear, non-transferable and beautiful memory.

If you were at least sorry about it! Lucia reproached me. If you could at least say sincerely that you were sorry, that you didn't mean it . . . Do you know what a relief that would be for me?

You are proud and stubborn! You won't admit that you made a mistake. You did make a mistake after all. Everyone is expecting you to apologize, Jarka . . .

But I never regretted what I did, only what I didn't do. What I didn't have the courage to do.

I went into the hut, took off my shoes, put the things I had brought from home on the table. I lay down on the cardboard that was spread on the floor, put my head on my rolled-up sweatshirt and covered myself with the second blanket. We slept almost the whole night through. Just before dawn I woke up suddenly, something had disturbed me, but it wasn't a sound or hunger, it was something inside me. For a moment I didn't know where I was, I thought I was lying at home in the hallway among the things from the black garbage bags. Then my eyes fell on the bed and Christian's leg. I got up and went over to the bed. The boys were sleeping deeply and when I stroked their faces with my finger, they didn't even move.

Adele wasn't sleeping. But she wasn't moving either. Her eyes were half-open, her arms bents at the elbow and placed on the blanket that was up against Christian's shoulder and she wasn't doing anything, just lying there quietly. I took her carefully in my arms, she seemed light and flimsy like something without a backbone. She leant on me, looked into my face. I lifted her such that I could kiss her on the cheek. She was hot, her face was sort of transparent and her breathing shallow. If she hadn't run her eyes over my face, there would be nothing to convince me that she was alive.

I knew that something had happened. Something bad. From how she was looking at me, how her arm fell limp when I let it drop. Something was wrong with her even if she wasn't coughing, bleeding or crying. Then I was gripped by horror, my chest tightened and my heart started to rip up that terror and pump it throughout my body.

A memory involuntarily came up in my head of one afternoon when Lucia didn't come to pick me up at pre-school. I sat on the carpet in the middle of the room, which looked suddenly empty, without children and toys—enormous and vaulted like a cave. I sat on the carpet and held some blocks in my hands that didn't go together, blocks from incomplete sets, sets that you couldn't put together. The teacher walked around me, collecting the last toys from the floor and putting them on the shelves. You couldn't hear her at all. Maybe she had taken off her slippers, maybe she was walking like a ghost, a finger's length above the earth. Then she sat down at the desk and started writing something. She didn't notice me, she forgot about me, forgot that she had stayed at work longer because of me and was doing what she didn't have time to do on other days. Nothing linked us together, even the green carpet ended two steps from her desk. I sat there like an obedient child who had been kept after school. I kept hearing the banging of lockers and all those children leaving, chattering and yelling, even though the last ones had left a little less than an hour before. I imagined it was night, I was sleeping on the carpet in the middle of a dizzyingly large classroom and under my head was the pillow from the pram. The teacher left me in this state of terror for two hours and then took me home. Lucia was sleeping after a night shift.

Then Adele moved a little, she turned her head and closed her eyes. I looked into her face for a long time and said to myself that everything was all right, that some children are simply quieter and calmer than others. I repeated to myself that no one had ever died of a fever. A raised temperature is normal after all, I had got over or slept through one a hundred times.

Maybe I was just watching Adele too much. I myself was tired and sleep-deprived, all sorts of things were coming to mind.

I preferred to put her down to sleep next to Christian and try to fall asleep myself. It was, hard, though, for me to keep my eyelids closed and not think about her.

It began to get light and I didn't know whether I had slept or not. I just suddenly realized that the sky was growing light and taking on some colour. I sat down at the table, ate a candy bar and several spoonfuls of Nutella and sat there quiet as a mouse. I wondered how we would spend the day which, judging from the clear sky outside, might be lovely and without rain. I looked at Adele. Once again, she looked alright, like a normal, sleeping child.

At half past six Christian woke up because he suddenly fell out of bed. It was so funny! I laughed with my hand over my mouth, I sputtered and hiccupped, and Christian didn't even have a chance to groan. He was still naked. He awoke just as he had fallen asleep, he didn't realize it. He sat on the floor, hunched over and weak, his eyes blinking and his pee-pee becoming slightly erect. Looking at his funny figure, at his tiny, stiff little organ lifted my mood.

I handed him his things and took a spoonful of Nutella for him. Without a word he got dressed, licked the spoon and sat down on the bed. He looked like a heap of unhappiness, numb and offended by my laughter. He didn't say anything, just looked around the room and rubbed his feet together and I had the feeling that, suddenly, he didn't like our household anymore.

Mama makes me tea in the morning, he said after a moment without looking at me. A clear reproach. Now you have to make it yourself, I said to him. My laughter had passed, the joy had disappeared. Again, there sat a small, helpless, grumpy boy in front of me. He started to pull at his nose and hunch over so much that his face wasn't visible. OK then, I'll make it for you. But I only have apple tea, I said. I don't drink that kind, he answered. You drank it yesterday. No, I didn't. I remember it. I would never drink that kind. You're lying. So then I changed my mind again, sat back down in the chair and ate three more spoonfuls of Nutella.

He didn't know what to do, because in the garden hut there wasn't anything to anchor his morning. He didn't have his cup, his toilet, his teddy bear, vitamins, four peeled apple quarters on a plate, he couldn't see his father's departing car through the window, couldn't hear the radio. He almost burst into tears. I sat down by him and stroked his head. I put my arm around his shoulders. He didn't resist for long, only a split second, until he felt my warmth and admitted to himself that he wouldn't get any other kind of warmth this morning. He relaxed and buried his face in my T-shirt. You should go home, Christian, I told him, but he shook his head.

You should go home, Christian, I said to him again, but not very convincingly. He would definitely feel good at home, that's for sure. He would get everything he needed for this new day in his life to begin as it should. That is, everything that I could not provide him. No herbal tea with honey, poppy-seed cake, apple without seeds, a clean towel, a toothbrush and miniature hourglass clock thanks to which he knew how long to brush. Nor a view of his daddy's car in the curve of the road, or that look at Mama a minute later, Mama who was listening to the Slovak Radio weather forecast with her ear to the speaker. Both of them as precise as a wristwatch. Satisfied that everything is working smoothly, all the parts are working towards a total synchronicity of the whole, even if they are far from each other and each one is driven by his or her own motor, own ambitions and images of life. Every day is sooth-ingly the same, it begins like the one before it and ends like the one after it. In our household, of course there was nothing of that.

Something is wrong with Adele, I said. She has a fever. While you were sleeping, I went home and got some medicines. Do you know how to read, Christian? I asked pouring all the blister packs and leaflets onto the bed. He looked at me a bit disbelieving and offended and began to dig around in the medicines, as if he'd never seen anything like them before. That's because he had actually never seen anything like that. At home, they had the medicines locked in a cupboard, a cup-board with a child-lock on it so that Christian couldn't get to them. When he was supposed to take something, they gave it to him through a straw or mixed it into some juice so that he never even noticed it.

It says on these papers which medicine is for fevers. Find it. I'll look in the bag. There are some bottles there, I said, rummaging in a bag. Subsimplex, I read out loud. Vigantol. I don't know what those are. You read aloud too if you want. And watch the children. They're sleeping. That's good.

A-s-p-ir-in. Use-cau-tion-when-oper-at-ing-a-mo-tor-ve-hi-cle or u-sing-hea-vy-ma-chin-ery. Machinery? Christian had begun to read word for word from the middle of the leaflet. I burst out laughing and Christian also smiled a bit and, encouraged, read the other side of the leaflet too. E-ffects-of-tri-o-tri-o-ti-ro-ni-nu-io-tirpo-lio-ni-nu-which-heals . . . hmm, I don't understand, he mumbled and read further to himself, only his lips moving. I don't understand this at all . . . he whispered and looked unhappily at the leaflet. De-no-xi-nal-60-T-B-L. I took the leaflet from his hands and read aloud. Supports liver detoxification function and protects it from damage . . . has a cleansing influence on the bloodstream . . . helps eliminate toxic substances from the body . . . hmm, this should be good, I think . . . but find something where they mention fever, or temperature. There has to be something like that.

Christian read attentively and I matched the leaflets with the medicines.

You were at home? He asked suddenly. Yes. When? While you were sleeping. I didn't notice. You were sleeping like a log. Hmm. Why? You were tired, no? I don't know. No, no . . . Why did you go home? Ah ha . . . we need medicine don't we. And clothes. You destroyed my sweatshirt. Ah ha. Sorry, I didn't mean to . . . , he said, and I knew that he really was sorry.

He sat there quiet for a moment twisting his finger around in an empty pill hole in one of the blister packs. At my house

. . . he began with a different voice, which he meant to sound careless . . . the lights were on, I said, interrupting him. They're looking for you. But don't worry, they won't find you here . . . Mama . . . I didn't see her. Don't think about her, OK? And try to find me the Faxiprol. Fa-xi-prol.

Christian looked for the medicine, announcing the names in a whispering voice. Adele started to whimper, so I made her some milk with the rest of the warm water that was left in the pot. Adele refused the milk, shaking her head from side to side and waving her fists, but her movements lacked energy and force. In the end, I managed to put the nipple into her mouth and get some milk into her. I picked her up and carried her around the room for ten minutes so that she would burp. She fell asleep on my shoulder, her arms hanging down over my elbows. A drop of milk quietly flowed from the corner of her half-open mouth. Her breathing was shallow.

I didn't say anything, but it was as if Christian could read my mind and also starting to feel fear or some kind of premo- nition. He put the leaflets in a pile and lay the blister packs next to each other such that he could read the names easily, but his eyes kept wandering to the child. He began to sing, a bit of some popular evening fairytale. He sang to himself, qui- etly, with his head bent way down. The song was only inter- rupted by the announcement of the medicine names, which were too long, or couldn't be read because of the ripped blister packs. Nonetheless, it seemed to me that Christian was singing too loudly, I could hear him clearly, singing lyrics, which he didn't know, because they didn't actually exist. The song didn't have any words, it was just a melody, just some hmmm . . .

hummm . . . hummmm . . . Some words emerged in my head like clouds and then disappeared again without me understanding what they meant.

Have you found anything? No. I don't get this stuff, it's confusing. Hm. We can't just give her anything without knowing what it is. Do you remember that Eighth Grader who lives on Maple Street, who took some pills on a trip and they had to pump her stomach at the hospital? Do you know how sick she was? They said she almost didn't survive, that she was totally blue, I remembered, but Christian didn't remember anything. He wasn't in school yet then and hadn't heard anything about that girl from Maple Street. I didn't know anything more either, but everyone said that they had pumped her stomach. Or something like that. How do they do that? How should I know? I don't know.

She should go to the hospital, said Christian suddenly. Definitely. He said definitely, but he wasn't convinced, he wasn't sure enough of himself to make proposals and offer solutions. Usually he just followed orders that were given to him sensitively and with a smile, as a request. I was quiet.

My mother always took me to the hospital when I had a fever. Even at midnight, to the emergency room, by ambulance, he said, defending himself. I had never been to the hospital because of a fever, a temperature, that's nothing. You could just get through it by being in bed. By sweating it out. It always passed by itself, I said objecting. I almost died, really. Don't talk nonsense Christian, you can't die from a fever. Yes, you can. Well, all right you can die. I'm not going to argue with you. Just forget about it, Christian, OK? Are you hungry?

Quiet, just a barely noticeable shaking of the head. Christian! Yes? Forget about it, OK? Stop it, you're getting on my nerves. That harping.

I'll go with her, he said after five minutes of silence during which he laced his fingers in between Adele's like a rosary. What? I'll take her. Where? To the hospital. Are you crazy? She doesn't feel well. Yes, she does. No, she doesn't! You can't go! You're not going anywhere, Christian. What kind of idiocy is this, you can barely even carry her around. Yes, I can. No, you can't. And stop arguing with me. I can carry her there . . . I carried the groceries up here . . . his chin began to tremble, but he controlled himself, raised his head and looked me straight in the eye, for the first time since I'd taken him off the tram. I'll take her there, he said decisively, his fists clenched, his jaw set.

OK, I said. No, no, it's stupid. I'll go. If that's what you really want . . . but only to make you happy, I said.

Christian had eroded my confidence, but I didn't want to admit it in front of him. After all, I remembered well how sick I had felt when I lay in bed with a fever sweating, the sweat soaked into my pyjamas and the bedcovers and I couldn't even stand up or crawl or even turn down the bedcovers. And Lucia kept bringing me water and made me drink and lie under that horrible, damp cover. She herself sat in front of the television eating popcorn. In the morning, my temperature had come down and by evening I was all right again, just very weak and groggy.

I've been for intravenous fluids at the hospital too, said Christian interrupting my thoughts again. With those snaky tube things, I couldn't move from the bed for three days because I was tied to a bottle. Water dripped from it and went through the snake tube straight into me. It was a long time ago, Mama told me about it.

OK then. But you'll stay here alone with Jacob, Christian. By yourself, do you understand? You'll have to take care of him and be careful that he doesn't cry so that no one hears you. There are always people walking through the vineyards, some men, probably homeless people. So be careful and go out only when the little one is quiet. Understand? I understand.

I wanted to put her in the carriage, but when I saw how big and garish the carriage was and how muddy the road was, I decided to leave it behind the hut. I put the baby in the large bag that they had with them when I took them from the station. The bag was big, and Adele fit comfortably inside with her knees bent. Meanwhile, Christian had cleared away the medicines, made some extra milk and put it into his backpack along with Adele's clothes, nappies and several toys. He was restless and tried to hide it by doing something useful. He flew around the room like a housefly doing all kinds of things, pushing in the chair, blowing crumbs off the table, looking into the bag, looking out the window. At six o'clock, with the big, heavy bag hung across my chest and Christian's backpack on my back, I left the garden and set off down the hill. I knew that Christian was standing by the window watching as I walked through the damp grass and tried to find the right position for carrying the bag without crushing the child inside it or falling down. I didn't wave to him, or even look back, because then I would risk turning around and returning.

The sun was coming out, the city was in front of me, behind me the steamboat in a sea of grass. The smokestacks of the refinery, the tyre factory, the roof of the stadium grandstand, the raised rail bed, the vocational school for chemists, everything at my fingertips. I peeked into the bag, and with my hand felt the sleeping child who seemed to get heavier and heavier.

I scampered down the hill as fast as I possibly could, and down the familiar road among the garages and family houses where the people were only just waking up. I met a smiling woman with a dog and a man who was scraping a highway sticker off the front windshield of his car. Beyond the railway bridge, the street became unpleasantly full of people and the tempo much faster. I walked along the tram tracks and wondered what I would do if Adele woke up in the tram and started to cry. I would start to cry too so that she couldn't be heard, I guess that's what I'd do. It reminded me of a scene from a film that, thanks to my eccentric mama, I had seen as a child.

The tram stop was full of people. I slowed down and thought. I looked over the people, trying to guess what they were thinking about and whether I stood out too much.

An older woman with a grocery bag on wheels looked at me for a moment and then took her eyes off me. She was exactly like Irena . . . Jarka, run to the store and buy some rolls, run, so you can be one of the first . . . before the rolls are all crushed and picked over. The woman grasped the bag in one hand and held her sweater closed with the other; it had one buttonhole that was stretched out and the button kept coming undone. Suspicious, cross, impatient. A few metres from the stop, when I was already so close that I could tell what colour her button was, my ankle suddenly turned and I, as if against my will, stepped off the pavement onto the tram tracks. I crossed to the pavement on the other side, waited calmly for the green light. Then, I crossed the four-lane street on the crosswalk. I felt like running, but I didn't, I walked in a carefree way, as if I took this route every day. Every day at a quarter to seven, with a big bag and a backpack, all by myself. I no longer noticed the weight of the bags at all, I didn't think about their contents, I just walked with discipline along the road, letting my intuition lead me.

A sleepy housing complex, the open doors of a delivery truck parked in front of the night grocer's, three black-haired children jumping on cardboard boxes in the yard of the Vietnamese boarding house. A monotonous voice of some kitchen appliance, the wash of sound from cars, trains, trolley-buses, people, electric current pulsing through wires, rodents, radios, spoons clinking in cups, papers falling in the hallway. On the road in the distance there was only one car and the first yellow leaves floating in shallow puddles, the reflection of an approaching September. A key, which slid into the lock with suspicious ease.

Lucia was sleeping in her bed. Without make-up and with clean skin, calm, rested, pink-cheeked. One of her arms was under the pillow, the other hung over the edge of the bed, her legs were tangled in a light summer bedcover. She had lovely tanned arms and long thin fingers with pronounced knuckles, no polish on her nails. She was beautiful. I looked at her for a while and said to myself that I would like to look something like that when I'm big. Like Lucia, when she's having a nice dream at the end of summer.

She was lying on the left side of the double bed, and the right side was empty. I turned back the second bedcover and put the bag on the sheet. Adele wiggled and whimpered weakly. Lucia didn't wake up, just moved her fingers slightly. I took the backpack off my shoulders and brought it into the kitchen. Then I took Adele a bit clumsily out of the bag and put her in the empty place next to Lucia. She was as limp as a ragdoll. I gave her some milk to drink that Christian had made, wiped off the stuff that ran down her chin and her pudgy neck. I put a rattle into her warm hand. When she woke up a little more and moved the rattle, Lucia would wake up and take care of her. She is a real mama, after all, she'll know exactly what to do with a sick baby.

Adele was in the bed, in the flat in the complex, surrounded by the civilized world, hot water, a gas stove, a bathroom. Adults were within reach. Familiar things—the television, tea kettle, clean towels, Lucia's ointments on the night table—occupied their normal places, it was enough to reach for them blindly and touch them.

I took the things out of the backpack and put them into the bag and left the bag on the kitchen table so that Lucia would notice it right away. From the full refrigerator I took a yogurt and ate it leaning against the doorframe with the unmade bed in view. I felt like lying down for a moment between them, just to rest. But I didn't want to wake Lucia, I didn't want to explain anything to her. At least I looked at her for a while. Like this, with the other half of the bed full of something living, she looked even better. If we had lived in a trio like this from the beginning, everything could have been different, I thought to myself. I finished the yogurt, wiped my mouth with my hand and kissed Adele on the forehead. I never saw her again.

The way back was fast and joyous. With an empty backpack on my back and a clear conscience, I ran out the entranceway and diagonally across the yard. At the moment when I pulled both feet from the ground at once, so that I could jump over some mud by the garbage dumpsters, Christian's father's car backed out from behind a parked trailer. With a loud slap my hands hit his back windshield. Through it I could see Christian's green car-safety seat. The car stopped, but only until Christian's father, from behind the glass, was convinced that I was still moving and had jumped back again. Far back enough so that I could do anything, open the door, bang on the window, run a key over his hood. The car gunned its engine immediately and furiously and took off. When he had backed up onto the main road, he stepped hard on the accelerator so that he could avoid an approaching delivery truck. The tyres squealed, leaving two skid marks on the road. It's exactly seven-fifteen, I thought to myself.

Christian's mother was standing in the window holding a small radio with an antenna to her ear. She was standing in the sitting room, in an almost transparent nightgown, pale and suffering but still beautiful. She probably hadn't slept all night.

Maybe she'd been sitting by the telephone waiting for some news, maybe she'd been walking around the complex looking for Christian, along with her family and neighbours with whom she'd been for the first time since they'd moved in, forced to communicate with them. Until then she hadn't even imagined how many people could fit into such a building.

She was always the exact opposite of Lucia, looking balanced and calm, elegantly dressed, no needless jewellery or movements, no gushing emotions. In her presence you wanted to do good, keep your voice down or doze. She was bulletproof, so perfect that it pissed you off. The neighbours were afraid to talk to her, because she looked like she had no interest. In the beginning, many people thought she was a foreigner, that she spoke some strange language and thus it was useless to approach her. Everyone who met her felt that this woman wasn't living in the right place. That she dreamt about a wellkept house with a garden in front and a safe, private play area, about a second child and passion that would some day return and settle in for at least one night a month between her and her husband. On her face you could see badly hidden disgust at the pieces of broken furniture piling up, the bags of garbage and the drunk neighbour lying by the dumpsters.

There was always a breeze around Lucia, shot glasses hopped on the table, the curtains billowed, words fell on the ground like stones. They were two different species. Nevertheless, at that moment the two women looked alike. Christian's mama hadn't yet brushed her hair and it was flying around and sticking to the velvet curtains, burning around her head like flames, the same as Lucia's hair spread out on the pillow. In the transparent nightgown she was almost naked. There was a moment when she took the corner of the curtain and covered her breasts with it. Fatigue and stress made her soigné beauty closer to the well-rested and worry-free face of my wrung-out mama. They could lie next to each other and look like two peas in a pod, smooth, perfect to the eye and touch, sprouts inside them.

Without my heavy and hot load, I felt light. I ran intermittently and jumped over puddles, I ran needlessly on a red light across the big intersection, under the railway bridge with closed eyes and among the garages in a carefree trot. I imagined Lucia waking up to the sound of a rattle, how she would jump out of the bed and run naked around the flat, return to the bed and, with disbelief, take the child in her arms. I laughed. In my laughter there was smugness and relief.

The vineyards that spread haphazardly up the slopes of the Small Carpathians were somehow strange that morning. The air was clear after the rain and without dust, the sky almost white. Coolness and calm were emanating from the ground.

The soil was soaked with water after the rain during the night, the old acacia posts creaked in the wind and grapes hung on the wires. The sky had cleared, water ran down the asphalt road. I had to watch where I was going so as not to step in the mud. I felt good, light, I was excited to see the boys, and along the way I picked four bunches of unripe grapes for Christian. Cold and covered with dew. I regretted not having brought anything from home for my beloved boys, we had an unusually full refrigerator.

Only one car passed me, an old Skoda with a gas tank full of holes that left an odour of petrol hanging in the air after it was gone. A freight train passed through the station, and then shortly afterward a fast train was announced. By the time I had slogged my way up the path between the gardens, the wind had come up and blown in some heavy, dark grey clouds. Suddenly it grew dark, cooled down and my intoxication from the beautiful morning disappeared. The grass was slippery, my tennis shoes were soaked—they'd been wet for a long time, but it only began to bother me now. I cursed silently to myself, broke off a twig from a rain-covered hibiscus that was growing over the fence of a garden, and threw it aside right away, because this needless thing in my palm gave me no pleasure. I thought about lunch. We could make something sweet, crepes or something like that, I guessed we could manage crepes in our improvised kitchen, crepes with Nutella, if Christian hadn't gobbled it up yet. We would deserve it—we had a difficult night behind us. Christian could go look for some fruit in the surrounding gardens, I would make the batter in the meantime. Or he could cut part of the garden grass under the tree with the small scythe with the wooden handle, so that we'd have somewhere to put down a blanket. We'd feel good out in the air, all three of us. If it didn't start to rain again. If it started to rain, we'd have to think of some other way to have fun. We could really clean up. Two of us could move the bed and lift the stove; Christian might be able to knock in the board that had come off the outer wall of the hut or straighten the posts that the gate hung on.

I had grand plans. If we had enough time, strength and tools, we could cut the grass in the whole garden, take out the wandering stones, even make some kind of swinging net out of the sheets and ropes where all three of us could rock. Instead of sitting around making smoke inside, we'd make a fire pit outside—we'd use the stones that we now just trip over. We would paint the roof and maybe even the walls of the hut. In spring we would plant something that doesn't need much care, some fruit bushes or strawberries. To start, though, it would be enough to make the crepes.

The gate was wide open, and the posts really did seem like they were leaning into the garden more than when I left. Instinctively I slowed down, started to move my feet so that I wouldn't drag the soles against the stones. I crouched down and looked through a hole in the hedge. I didn't see anything, but heard some chafing, creaking and clinking, like when bottles bang together inside a bag.

My heart began to beat quickly. I immediately dropped down and put my hands on the ground. Under my fingers I felt how cold the ground was after a long night of rain and it flashed through my head that one day the Earth will go completely cold, from the inside—its whole core will grow stiff as a stone. The roots of plants and trees, worms and rodents will remain imprisoned in their holes.

I listened. The rubbing and clinking stopped for a moment, but then I heard a creaking and a gurgled voice that I didn't understand. Two or three short syllables, nothing more. It could even be Christian, or the baby. Again, the clinking and rustling of the grass, and then something moving. The sound was quiet and commonplace, it could have come from a sleepy cat, or a stray dog. The clinking and creaking were hardly audible now. The wooden posts creak in the vineyards, the trees creak, the whole hut creaks. The tops of the compote jars and the pieces of tin hanging from the flowering trees in some gardens clink. When there's a strong wind, the two circular pressed coins hanging on the window frame of our garden hut clink too, I said to myself. There was something in the garden, something walking around.

It occurred to me that the black cat could be digging its way out of the ground. But no, the cat is stiff as a board, in two pieces—the motorcycle ran over him.

When all the sounds were quiet for a moment, I stood up, adjusted the straps of my backpack full of grapes and looked inside.

Two men were standing in the garden. One had high, olive-green rubber boots on—the creaking—the other had tennis shoes—the rustling. The one in the tennis shoes was carrying a plastic bag with bottles inside—the clinking. The bottles were full and the man was leaning to one side for balance. He was thin and bony, his clothes hung on him like a hanger.

The man in the rubber boots was looking around. He was tall and powerful and there was moderation and a carefree feeling about his movements. He was pulling up grass that happened to get tangled in his fingers and then letting it fall to the ground, his hands swinging freely by his sides. Sweat glistened on the nape of his neck, the sleeves of his light-coloured shirt were unbuttoned and rolled up just below the elbow and it occurred to me that it might be Peter. For a moment I forgot myself and almost took a step forward. I wanted to take a stalk of grass from in between his fingers, put my hand in his and walk with him to the hut accompanied by the squeaking of his boots and the clinking of the bottles. Just as I had walked through the freshly fallen snow in the winter dream.

Just then, the man with the plastic bag mumbled something under his breath and I froze with one leg in the air. Four deep ruts ran through the grass.

In the window something moved, but it was only a shadow, maybe not even that, maybe I only imagined it, I didn't have a good view of it, and I was too far away. There was no smoke coming out of the chimney, and no baby's crying to be heard, no sounds at all.

I didn't know what to do, I was drawing a complete blank, banal details were whizzing through my head in fast succession. That I still hadn't bought a tracksuit for gym class, that I would like a turquoise one with a hood. That at that moment Dorota was travelling down the Croatian coast where Lucia never took me. Lucia had looked really good that morning, like a fairy at the full moon. The grapes in my backpack would be crushed, bleed through the backpack and leave a stain on my back. If I had hung it in front on my chest, it would look like I had thrown up on myself. The button of that fake-Irena old lady and Christian's green car seat.

The men walked around the hut. The one in the boots stopped in front of the doors, stood with his feet apart, pulled up another stalk of grass and broke it into centimetre-long pieces between his fingers. The thin one walked up to the window, cupped his hands on the glass and looked inside.

I can't see anything, it's dark in there. There isn't anyone there anymore, he said loudly and stepped back. An hour ago, I saw that boy here and heard some crying. I'm sure, he added more quietly and scratched himself behind the ear.

With a broad gesture, the man in the boots threw away the bent stalk of grass and opened the door of the hut. Smoke poured out of it. The man let go of the handle and waved the smoke away from his face with his arms. Where are the keys? flashed through my head. Who has them? And what is all that smoke?

At that moment Christian jumped out from behind a metal barrel with the air rifle in his hands and a savage expression on his face. He looked like someone had made him appear, someone with their own specific sense of humour. He was wearing my T-shirt, a short T-shirt with a girl's cut and decorated with an appliqué, his underwear and thin white legs with knees like big knobs in the middle of them were sticking out from underneath. He was barefoot because he had lost one of his tennis shoes the day before. The air rifle trembled in his hands, a big, heavy weapon without ammunition, and he trembled with it. He held it as far away from his body as he could, and he didn't know what to do with it. He'd never seen a film where there was shooting.

Nothing changed in the carefree attitude of the man in the rubber boots, the other man let himself be pulled down to one side by the clinking bag, which he had not let go of the whole time. For a moment they stood like that facing each other, a silent dialogue taking place between them.

Put that air rifle down on the ground, said the man in the boots out loud after a moment. You'll hurt someone, he said with a bit of ridicule. The man with the bag gave a wheezy laugh, the bottles in the bag clinked.

Idiots, I said to them in my head. You don't know what he has inside, you don't know all the things that boy can do. He's totally different from what you think, idiots.

But I didn't do anything. I stood behind the bush as quiet as a mouse and prayed that neither of them would turn their head and see me. I didn't do anything at all, I left him by himself, I didn't stand behind him, didn't help him hold the air rifle that was dragging him down to the ground.

Where are the keys? It flashed through my head again, again something unimportant. It didn't matter at all where the keys were. Even if the door had been locked, they could have pried it open with two fingers. Where did I leave the keys? Where is the baby? Where did he hide the baby?

I ran my eyes over the garden, the narrow part that I could see from my position. The grass was now only shining in the shade of the trees, the branches laden with water were still dark and heavy. Nothing was moving anywhere, not even one leaf was swaying, neither Christian nor the men moved. The man in the boots didn't repeat his advice and Christian had managed to freeze with bent knees and the rifle butt propped between his ribs such that he wasn't wobbling anymore. Christian was pale, as if all the blood had drained out of him.

Then, suddenly, he bared his teeth and leapt forward with the air rifle in his hand. With unexpected agility he ran around both men and jumped through the tall grass all the way to the gate. There he stopped for a moment because the gun strap had got caught on the gatepost. He looked at me, I was standing a metre from him, but I had the feeling that he didn't see me at all, as if the point he was aiming for was kilometres away. He pulled hard on the rifle, pulled the strap free and ran off up the road. He tripped on a stone, the gravel piled up on the sides of the road crunched under his step and the mud stuck to the bottoms of his feet. He fell twice, his face hitting the cold, muddy grass, he dropped the rifle twice. After a while he disappeared among the fences.

The thin man hesitantly put the bag down on the ground and looked at the one in the boots. Should I catch him? He asked. No need, said the other one calmly and went into the house. As if nothing had happened, as if a moment ago, only a stray mutt had run by. The thin one shrugged his shoulders and looked regretfully at the gate. When they disappeared like thin smoke, I ran in front of the gate and ran after Christian. But the earth had swallowed him up. It was possible to follow his tracks up to the point where I had seen him turn, but then they just vaporized, he and his footprints. I wandered among the gardens, walked through terraced vineyards, looked for footprints in the mud. I felt like now I had to find Christian and deal with the rest of it later, because only I knew his fears, his fingers, because now we belonged together.

I walked back and forth through the vineyards and gardens. I heard a siren and the loudspeaker announcing the train arrivals. I walked bent over, stopping only at the crossroads of well-worn paths. It started to get warmer and I felt hungry. I ate some blackberries and grapes, a bunch from each vineyard, all different sorts. Christian had disappeared. I went into the woods, up the hill, I walked around for some time in an unfamiliar forest until I happened to come upon an asphalt road. The asphalt road led me out into the light, into civilization, to the tram stop. I rode two stops to the station, where I got off, scraped the layer of mud off my soles and went home.

When Lucia woke up about half an hour after my departure, she found a strange baby lying next to her. She put on her robe, some pumps, wrapped the baby in a blanket and rang Christian's mother's doorbell. Because Christian's mama—she was still standing by the window with the radio to her ear—was the first one Lucia saw when she looked terrified out her window searching for some clue.

She looked like an angel in that window, Lucia told me a few days later. Like a nurse from the children's cancer ward. Kind and capable. Nothing else occurred to me at that moment. I needed to get rid of that thing as quickly as possible. I wanted to wake up next to someone totally different. He was supposed to be there, he was supposed to wait for me. He promised me, but then he left before I woke up, she said sullenly.

Confused, Lucia then calls the man who had left her too early. He advises her to take the baby somewhere quickly, to someone trustworthy, that he is coming back right away, as soon as he takes care of some work stuff. He'll come back to her, just don't let there be a screaming child in the flat.

In the window opposite—like in a mirror—stands a woman with a slightly bowed head, listening constantly, like a sleepwalker, to the radio. Lucia knows that that woman is the mother of my friend.

After a little while they meet. They sit for five minutes in the sitting room, Lucia drinks coffee—really good coffee, high class, rich like velvet, you know what I mean, Jarka?—and admires her dusty-rose nightgown. She tries to explain to the woman what she wants from her. The angel-woman liberates her, takes the baby from her and sends her back home to get some sleep. A few minutes later a wailing ambulance pulls up. For a moment it wanders around the parking lot and then finally drives diagonally across the yard. The neighbours lean out of their windows—they cannot understand how Christian could have shrunk so much. Christian's mama presses the baby to her breast and doesn't want to let it go, even into the ambulance. Lucia watches the whole thing from behind closed curtains.

An hour after the ambulance comes, the man comes too, and Lucia forgets about the child very quickly. About all the children in the world. The man makes love to her again and lets her sleep, calm, hot and wet.

I find her in the same position that I had left her in, except the right side of the bed is empty again. On the kitchen table there is no bag with baby things in it, just the traditional cup of half-drunk coffee and an empty cigarette box. No trace remained from the short stay of a strange baby in our apartment.

I look for Adele, but Adele isn't there. She's not in my room, in Lucia's room, in the bathroom or in the hall, she's nowhere. The bed is messy, Lucia's still sleeping. I don't know what to think, I'm tired from all of this, from this endless walking in the vineyards, from the stress and fear. I cannot understand where the baby is, how she could disappear along with her things without Lucia waking up. There is nothing to demonstrate that Lucia's got up from the bed, everything is in its place. I don't know what to do. I don't know what to hold onto. I have no idea what has happened to the other baby, or Christian. I don't know whether I have dreamt the whole thing or not.

I sit down on the couch. I turn on the television and turn down the sound, so that Lucia won't wake up. I watch music videos. The pictures change quickly, but I don't understand the pictures either, I can't concentrate. I'm still thinking about what could have happened while I was out. I decide that I will not talk about it. If Lucia doesn't mention the child, then I guess there was no child in our flat, and I imagined the whole thing.

Lucia wakes up after a while and behaves as usual. She throws on a shirt, sits down on the edge of the bed, crosses her arm over her breasts and rubs her shoulder. She yawns.

What are you watching? she asks. Nothing, I say. Turn the sound up, I can't hear anything. I turn the sound up, and the flat is filled with some slow black soul. Oh, turn that off, be so kind, she says annoyed. I look at her, but she looks like she

always does, like wilted nettles. Are you hungry? Take something from the refrigerator, she says, she herself taking out a
cold pudding with whipped cream. The pudding with its hat
of white whipped cream shakes on the spoon and Lucia
closely watches this movement. After the third or fourth
spoonful, she suddenly rises, walks to the window and quickly
pushes back the curtain. She looks over at the building opposite. She doesn't say anything, and I pretend to watch the
videos, but in reality, I'm hanging on her every word and
waiting to see what she'll say. She stands there for a moment
chewing on her finger, then she returns to the table and scrapes
out the rest of the pudding with the spoon. Have some, it's
good, she says, throwing the container into the trash bin, and
starts to get dressed. I have to go out now, wait for me here,
OK? I'll be about two hours, no more. Don't open the door
for anyone, she adds. I'll lock the door just in case.

She's gone before I can react. I hear the clicking of her
heels on the stairs and the clinking of my keys, which she
sticks in her pocket. I stay on the couch, turn up the volume.
After about a half hour, someone rings the doorbell, but I
don't even get off the couch to look through the peephole and
see who it could be. I fall asleep on the couch, and the remote-
control falls in-between the cushions. I fall asleep with the
thought that we should finally tie the remote to the couch with
a string, so that we won't have to look for it every day.

I have a dream. I'm standing in a boat, which looks like a
fairytale steamboat. It's blue with white stripes and its cabin
is a miniature replica of my garden hut. It has a chimney,

gutters, and one window with tinkling metal coins. That's how it would look more or less if Christian and I managed to finish our planned reconstruction.

It's a windless day and the boat is sitting motionless in the middle of a swimming pool. The surface is smooth, it's not raining, the leaves aren't falling from the trees, and the insects are staying on the sidelines. The swimming area is very dirty and shabby, and if the pool weren't full of water, you'd think it had been abandoned for years. The blue steamboat is sitting motionless in the middle of it like a mirage.

I walk two steps to the window, carefully, so that the boat doesn't rock too much, I lean over, press my forehead to the glass and cup my hands around my eyes so I can see. Inside everything is arranged like in my garden hut. There's a bed under the window, an iron stove, a table, cups on the shelves, and metal rivets shine on the window frame. An amiable and cosy room for a recluse. I wonder how it's possible that all these things fit into such a small space.

I return and climb over the railing. I sit down on the edge of the boat, which is rocking a little. I dip the tips of my tennis shoes into the water, circles form on the surface. I move further towards the edge and submerge my legs above the ankles. I feel the water running into my tennis shoes and they get heavier. I close my eyes, and jump. I sink down under the water, just floating down for a moment, and then I swim a few quick strokes. My hair spreads out on the surface, ballooning up. I swim with eyes closed and think about the fact that in a moment I will hit the wall of the pool. But nothing like that happens. I swim on fast, and the wall of the pool keeps getting farther away from me. I'm still in the same pool, only I can't see to the end or the beginning of it. The boat has remained far behind me, I only see a blue dot now, and behind it a wide-open space, the cubes of changing cabins, the snack bar and the sky like a flat, steel-blue canvas. I go under and swim further without generating any energy. I become one with my outstretched arms, the current pulls me forward. I don't resist. I'm tired. When the current lets up for a moment, I sink to the bottom, lay my head down on my hands and fall asleep.

They searched for Christian and the baby with dogs and a helicopter. They found him the next day at dawn, not far from my garden. Maybe he'd been lost the whole time among the vineyards, like me, maybe he was sitting in a narrow concrete pipe full of water that served as a bridge between the road and the garden. He was chilled to the bone and had stopped speaking completely. I wanted to explain all kinds of things, hug him, tell him that he was brave, that he hadn't disappointed me. I wanted to hear from him how he had managed by himself in the garden. I was convinced that he would tell me everything. They stuck him in the hospital and didn't let any strangers in to see him. But I was no stranger.

I saw Christian some years later at a filling station. We sat opposite each other at a miniature aluminium table, next to a shelf full of jerry cans with windshield wiper fluid in them, both silent and puzzled.

Christian took after his father. He was tall, clumsy, well-dressed and well-behaved. He looked good from head to toe, but his movements were hesitant, as if he weren't sure whether the way he was lifting the cup to his lips was correct. He kept saying I'm not quite sure . . . I can't find the right words . . . I don't know whether you understand me...I would like to say it more precisely, but I can't find a good way . . . At times I felt like slapping him in the face, so that he would wake up. Like he had then, in the garden.

After those events, Lucia and I packed up and moved as quick as lightning. I bought myself a new tracksuit jacket in a completely different town, in a backwater where they turned off the streetlamps at midnight. I missed the trams, billboards, my room, Peter, the wide streets, the housing complex. Lucia was terrified that she would one day meet that unhappy woman from the station on the street and couldn't imagine that she would have to look at Christian's flat window every day and pass his mother in the parking lot. She couldn't stand the neighbours' looks, was afraid of journalists, police and social services. So, she preferred to leave our flat to a girlfriend, and we got off the boat with our bags on the first of September in front of some boarding house. From there, we left three months later and moved in with some elderly lady, into a room with a balcony. Then to a farm, then back to the woman and round and round.

Then one day Lucia fell into the brook. She took a sedative and got drunk.

I really had to try very hard not to hear her anymore. I had to fight hard not to feel her waking up inside me and whispering—Jarka, don't make trouble, there've been enough problems already, Jarka, don't ruin other people's lives. You creep into other people's lives, even if they don't want it. Jarka, why are you such a bad girl? Jarka, remember those babies . . .

The brook she fell into was shallow and flowed slowly and peacefully. In some stretches the surface barely moved, fallen willow leaves caught by the edges and spun in small vortexes. At one point the brook flowed under a bridge that was built out of a concrete pipe and iron crossties, at another it flowed under fallen willow trees. Beyond the bridges there were small plum orchards, beehives and pastures. It was a beautiful place at the end of a village in Central Slovakia. You would want to sit down on the bridge with your legs dangling down over the water, break off a stick and run it over the surface.

I don't know how she got there, why she was there when she had lived her whole like in cities larger or smaller. She preferred to walk on asphalt pavements, streetlamps that were on all night didn't bother her, she liked all-night grocers, strobe lights and blinking disco balls, coffee- vending machines and lifts. The cursed virgin in the River Vah, said the policeman who took me to the place. Over that hill are three or four chalets that are rented out in the summer . . . maybe she was celebrating something . . . young people like to come here to party, there's cheap booze here, every house distils its own and sells it through the cellar window . . . maybe she was dizzy . . . or she got lost, he wondered aloud. Are you her sister? He asked. Daughter, I said. It sounded strange. How old is she? Thirty-five. Hmm . . . pretty woman . . . he said with admiration.

Once when she was drunk, she had told me that only I was responsible for everything bad—what happened to Irena, Christian, Christian's parents, those two babies, their mother and their whole family. She spit it out, just like that, as an aside, like saliva. And I believed her, after all she was my mama. Since then, I've thought about all the people whose lives I ruined and tried not to interfere in anyone else's life, not to let anyone get so close enough for me to hurt them unintentionally.

Then in September, after an evening spent with Dorota and Peter, something happened all the same.

We sat for an hour in Peter's kitchen and listened to Dorota who could chatter without interruption for hours on end. When Dorota got up to leave, I went with her to the trolley-bus stop and came back. I stood for a long time on landing in front of her father's door and looked out onto the street. It was already dark and warm outside. I stood there a good ten minutes and looked through the half-open window at the outer staircase and its wrought-iron railing, the plastic bags bulging out of the full garbage cans. The street was empty, the windows in the houses opposite dark and deep like holes after a shooting. The people whom I had walked by a moment before were already home but hadn't yet turned on all the lights and the television. I hesitated and my strength drained out of me all at once. I had needed him as a child and now I needed him again. I leant against the wall and closed my eyes.

I gathered up my courage. I thought of the dinner we'd had, of the fog that had settled on us, the touch. I could have been mistaken, confused by the memories of those lovelier moments of my childhood, the feeling of safety and trust, of something so simple that no one else had been able to give me.

It was then that three boys of about ten years old walked by me. They were so absorbed in their own stuff that they passed me without even noticing me at all, without lowering their voices or moving aside. They were talking quietly and the tallest one stuttered. One of them was carrying in front of him, with outstretched arms, a cardboard box. In the box was a big black cat. It was dead. Another boy was jumping by the box and looking inside constantly. Since there were only private yards here and between the fences there were asphalt alleyways, there was no place to dig a hole for miles. Clearly, they should have been home long ago, but they had vowed that they would bury this cat come hell or high water, and I understood their decision. I had already buried my dead cat long ago.

At the moment they turned the corner and disappeared from my sight, the lights in three flats in the villa opposite went on at the same time. A sign. I told myself that if they all went out at the same time, I would go up and knock on the door without hesitating. Chance and hope converged at the discovery of an animal cemetery in Bratislava.

The door opened at the moment I wanted to knock with my knuckle. As if Peter had been waiting on the other side of the door with his hand on the handle. As if he'd been standing there the whole time I had been walking with Dorota to the stop and back.

Where were you until now? I asked myself silently. God, where have you been all my life? It wasn't a reprimand, it was sorrow for all the days we had missed. He didn't say anything. He looked a bit scared. We sat for a moment in the kitchen and Peter tracing the rim of a glass with a wet finger. Then he laid his hand on mine, just like he did in the car when I was it was my job to shift the gears. He smiled, he remembered it too. Then something shook me, like when an anchor is pulled up and the boat is slowly, but surely carried away by the current. I stood up, walked through the entire flat and turned off all the lights. I couldn't wait for something to happen that would forever interrupt this fragile link between us. I had to act before a wrench fell into the works, some enormous wrench that would get stuck there for another ten years.

I turned off all the lights and returned to the kitchen. It was empty. I looked for him in the dark, in a flat that was unfamiliar, drunk with his presence. The objects in the rooms had soft contours and breathed quietly like sleeping children. In each room I left a piece of my four-piece outfit. Then I heard quiet whistling. I found him and took the glass from his hand. He embraced me. I wasn't a little schoolgirl anymore. Where have you been? He asked.

At that moment Lucia fell silent. I couldn't believe how simple, quick and painless it was, suddenly.

The boys from the street were probably already at home scrubbing their hands in hot water. They had managed to bury the cat, had found some dignified place. Perhaps they'd jumped over the fence and stuck it under some poor cadaver sleeping in his crypt at Goat's Gate Cemetery. Now they will sleep well with the feeling that they've done a good deed without looking ridiculous, because even though carrying a bag up the stairs for Grandma is what you're supposed to do, for a ten-year-old it's embarrassing. In the morning they'll meet and wink at each other in a secret conspiracy, but they won't mention the black cat out loud.